Polly's First Year at Boa

Polly's First Year at Boarding School

by Dorothy Whitehill

CHAPTER I—THE FIRST DAY OF SCHOOL

Seddon Hall, situated on top of one of the many hills that lined either side of the Hudson River, was a scene of hubbub and confusion. It was the 27th of September and the opening day of school. The girls who had already arrived were walking arm in arm about the grounds, in the broad assembly hall, and in the corridors, talking, laughing and discussing the summer vacation, plans for the winter, the new girls, and a variety of subjects with fine impartiality.

In the Senior reception room Mrs. Baird, principal of the school, and a number of the faculty were receiving and assuring the mothers and guardians of the girls.

Outside the carriages from the 5:04 train were winding up the steep hill from the station. The girls were waving and calling hellos as they passed one another, and on the broad piazza there was a quantity of suit cases, and a good deal of kissing.

Polly Pendleton, seated beside her uncle in one of the last carriages, was just the least little bit frightened. She had never seen quite so many girls nor heard quite so much laughing and talking in all her rather uneventful life.

Polly's real name was Marianna, but her heavy dark hair framed a face so bright and full of fun, and her big brown eyes had so much impishness in their depth, that to have called her by anything so long and dignified seemed absurd, and so she had been Polly all her life.

Until two months before this story opens she had lived her thirteen years in an old fashioned New England town with her aunt, Hannah Pendleton, her father's eldest sister, and quite as severe as her name. It had been a very unexciting existence—school every morning with the village minister, and a patchwork "stint" every afternoon under the direction of Aunt Hannah.

Polly was beginning to think every day was going to be just like every other, when suddenly Aunt Hannah died and she came to New York to live with Uncle Roddy. It had been a great change to leave the old house and the village, but under Uncle Roddy's jolly companionship she soon ceased to miss any part of her old life.

After what seemed an age, the carriage finally reached the top of the hill, and Polly, holding tight to her uncle's arm, was shown into the reception-room. She was finding it harder every minute to keep down the unaccountable lump that had risen in her throat, when Mrs. Baird, catching sight of them, held out a welcoming hand.

"How do you do, Mr. Pendleton?" she asked. "And is this Marianna? My dear," she added, putting her hand on Polly's shoulder, "I hope you are going to be very happy and contented with us."

It was perhaps the fiftieth time Mrs. Baird had made that same remark that day, but Polly, looking into her kindly blue eyes, felt, as had every other new

3

girl at Seddon Hall, the complete understanding and sympathy of the older woman, and felt, too, without knowing why, that Mrs. Baird had had her first day at boarding-school.

Louise Preston, one of the Seniors, a slender girl of seventeen, with heaps of taffy-colored hair, big blue eyes, and the sweetest and jolliest smile, caught her principal's beckoning nod, and coming forward, was presented. Mrs. Baird suggested that she take Polly and show her to her room.

As the two girls mounted the broad staircase, Louise linked her arm in Polly's in a big sisterly fashion, and began the conversation.

"This floor that we're coming to," she explained, "is Study Hall floor; all those doors are classrooms. This is the Bridge of Sighs," she continued, stopping before a covered passage which led from one building to another.

"Why the Bridge of Sighs?" inquired Polly.

They were crossing it as she asked. When they reached the other side, Louise solemnly pointed to a door on the left.

"That," she explained, "is Miss Hale's room. Miss Hale is the Latin teacher, and when you know her, you'll understand why this is the Bridge of Sighs."

"Goodness! let's hurry past if she's as dreadful as all that," laughed Polly. "What's this long corridor?"

"This is the Hall of Fame or, in other words, the abode of the Senior class," Louise told her. "Junior and Sophomore corridors are in the other wing, and Freshman Lane, where you'll be, is just above this on the next floor. You see the classes are named as they are in college."

"Then who are the little girls I saw downstairs?"

"Those were the younger children; we don't see much of them until they're Intermediates—that's the class just before the Freshmen," Louise explained.

"Now we'll find your room."

When they reached the floor above, they were met with a shout of joy as the girls, who were dashing in and out of one another's rooms, caught sight of Louise.

"Hello, Louise, how are you? Awfully glad you're back," called some one. "Why didn't you answer my letter?"

"Don't you realize this is *Miss* Preston, that we're a dignified Senior this year, and we mustn't be called Louise?" corrected another laughing voice.

Then, as they caught sight of Polly, they stopped short. It was Louise who broke the embarrassed silence by asking:

"Does any one know where Marianna Pendleton's room is?"

At the unfamiliar sound of her real name, Polly looked so puzzled that she added:

"Your name is Marianna, isn't it?"

"Yes," assented Polly, "but I'll never get used to it. No one has ever called me anything but Polly."

"Then Polly you shall be; it suits you, and Marianna doesn't."

4

"How do you do? I'm Betty Thompson. Louise doesn't seem to have the manners to introduce me."

It was golden-haired, snub-nosed, freckled, little Betty, one of the most popular of the younger girls, who was speaking. Her timely impudence made every one laugh, and the ice was broken.

"I stand corrected," murmured Louise, in what was meant to be an abject voice. "I'll begin introducing you at once. This is Roberta Andrews; she's in your class. This is Constance Wentworth; we're very proud of Connie; she plays the piano wonderfully."

"But she talks in her sleep," interrupted Betty.

Everybody laughed at this. It was an old joke that Constance, when in the Intermediate class the year before, had frightened one of the poor new teachers almost to death by reciting Lady Macbeth's sleep walking scene, at twelve o'clock one night.

Polly liked her at once. There was something very beautiful about her firm mouth, straight nose, high cheek bones, and big, dreamy brown eyes.

"This is Angela Hollywood," Louise continued. "Don't take any stock in her name, it's deceiving."

Angela, who looked like an old-fashioned painting with her eyes as blue as the sky, her pink and white cheeks, and her soft ringlets of golden-brown hair, scowled threateningly.

"Your being a Senior," she drawled, "is all that saves you from my wrath." Then, turning to Polly, she continued: "Don't let her give you a wrong impression; you see, she's jealous. I really am quite angelic—"

"Do tell me when that is," demanded a voice from the other end of the corridor. The girls turned to look and there, standing with suit case and tennis racket in hand, dressed in a blue Peter Thompson sailor suit, her tawny-colored hair tied half way down her back with a black ribbon, her dark eyes dancing with fun, stood Lois Farwell.

Polly, standing to one side as the girls crowded around the newcomer, realized that in some way she was different from the other girls. The welcome she was receiving showed her to be a general favorite and much thought of. When in a few minutes she was shaking hands with her, she understood. Lois was evidently born to be liked.

The girls rattled on, asking a million questions at once. Louise left for the society of her own class, and Polly went to her room to unpack her case.

In a few minutes there was a knock at her door; one of the maids had come to tell her she was wanted in the reception-room to say good-by to her uncle. As she started down the corridor she met Lois.

"Where are you going?" questioned the latter. "Anything I can do for you?"

Polly tried hard to keep back the lump in her throat as she answered:

"I am going to the reception-room; my uncle is leaving."

"Better take me with you," Lois advised. "You'd never find your way alone."

When Polly reached the reception-room she found Uncle Roddy decidedly unhappy. He was feeling a responsibility for, perhaps, the first time in his bachelor life, and he didn't like it.

She said good-by to him, promised to write, and received his hug and kiss with a choked sensation. Something snapped as the carriage disappeared down the hill. She realized she was all alone. She would have given anything to have been able to run after the carriage and beg him to take her home with him.

The lump in her throat was asserting itself in tears as Lois came back to find her.

"Come on up to Assembly Hall and meet some of the girls," she suggested, putting her arm around her shoulder and pretending not to notice the tears. At this touch of comradeship the lump in Polly's throat, as if by magic, disappeared.

The rest of the day was a blur to Polly, as it was to all the new girls. As she lay wide awake in bed until late that night, she tried to form a clear idea of what had happened.

"I'm quite sure I'm going to like Angela and Connie," she said to herself. "And I adore Betty; she's such fun. But Lois is the nicest of all. It was awfully sweet of her to ask me to sit beside her for Mrs. Baird's welcome talk, and she's promised to take me over the grounds tomorrow.

"No one talked about anything I didn't understand, either, except basket-ball, and Betty's promised to teach me how to play that the first chance she gets."

Then she continued sleepily:

"Every one home used to say I was different from most girls, and Aunt Hannah said I was a tomboy. But I'm just like all the rest—just an ordinary girl."

And with a sigh of contentment she snuggled down in her pillows and dropped off to sleep to dream of the happy year to come.

CHAPTER II—THE PAPER CHASE

It was two o'clock in the afternoon and the end of the first school day. There had been no lessons to speak of. The new girls had been piloted to the various classrooms, introduced to the teachers, received their books and the general plan for the year had been laid out.

At the close of the last period Lois Farwell and Betty Thompson met in the Study Hall corridor, and locking arms, sauntered off in the direction of Freshman Lane.

"My, but it's good to be back again," began Betty, playing a tattoo with her pencil on the steam pipes, that ran along under the windows on one side of the corridor; "bully to be back," she repeated.

"Bet, do stop that fiendish noise," begged Lois. "You're as bad as ever. Yes, it is good to be back; what shall we do to celebrate?"

"Let's talk about the new girls," suggested Betty; "how do you like them so far?"

"I haven't talked to many of them, the ones in our corridor seem to be all right. I think I'm going to like Polly Pendleton a lot."

"Oh! she's a duck," Betty agreed. "I like her already. The others are nice, too, but there's something different about Polly, she's—"

"Yes, I know what you mean," Lois answered slowly. "She's more Seddon Hallish than the rest; she sort of fits," she continued, wrinkling up her forehead in an attempt to explain a state of being not exactly describable in words.

At this point, they stopped to survey the bulletin board, and as they stood reading the notices posted, they were joined by Louise Preston and Florence Guile, both in Peter Thompsons, the accepted dress of the school, but with their hair fixed on top of their heads, as befitted the two most important members of the senior class.

"We want you two," greeted Louise; "been looking for you everywhere; we're trying to get up a paper chase for this afternoon, some of the new girls are 'weepy,' and Mrs. Baird thinks their thoughts had better be diverted from home."

Betty assumed an attitude of deep dejection.

"I'd sort of hoped to spend the afternoon studying," she sighed, regretfully, "but of course I'll be a martyr for such a worthy cause."

"Thanks, dear, we do appreciate your sacrifice," laughed Florence, "and you, Lo, we can count on you I suppose, as it is a favor to Louise?"

Lois blushed and looked self-conscious. She had been rather extravagantly fond of Louise the year before, and it embarrassed her to be reminded of it.

"Yes, I'll come," she replied with a great show of indifference. "That is, if I can be one of the hounds."

"Of course you may, that's one of the privileges of an old girl," Louise assured her. "But we must hurry; will you two go up and get the Freshmen together! We start at three from the gym."

"What about the paper?" Betty inquired. "I'll get it for you if you like and find a laundry bag with a hole in it."

"Do, and we'll love you forever," promised Florence, adding over her shoulder as the two girls dashed off down the corridor:

"Be sure there's plenty of it, we want a long chase."

Three minutes later, breathless from their race upstairs, Betty and Lois reached Freshman Lane.

"Everybody ready for a paper chase at three o'clock," Lois called out; "no excuses need be offered for none will be accepted."

"Angela and Connie, you lazy ones, that means you, too, come along," Betty commanded, bursting into Connie's room and discovering her curled up comfortably on the bed, while Angela, sitting Turk fashion on the window seat, was devouring crackers and peanut butter sandwiches.

Pausing now with one half way to her mouth, she drawled:

"Oh, Betty, you're so energetic, I don't want to go, I'm much too tired."

She received no sympathy, however; instead, she was dragged ruthlessly to her feet and admonished:

"Too lazy you mean, and too full of peanut butter; no, Angela, it is my painful duty to save you from growing hideously fat." And Betty, as though the subject was settled, turned her attention to Connie. But Connie offered no opposition.

"I'll come with pleasure," she assured her. "Anything would be better than watching Ange stuff."

Lois had proceeded to some of the other rooms and found their occupants only too eager for something to do.

"I can't find Polly Pendleton," she called as Betty joined her, still holding tightly to the reluctant Angela. "Have you seen her?"

Some one called out that she had not returned to her room after school, so Lois went down to the Study Hall, in search of her.

She met her half way up the stairs.

"Were you looking for me?" she asked. "Louise Preston told me that there was to be a paper chase and that you'd tell me what to do."

"Oh good, then you know," answered Lois. "Come on back to the corridor," she suggested; and slipping her arm around Polly's shoulder, asked:

"You're not homesick, are you!"

Polly smiled curiously, and half closed her eyes.

"Not now," she answered truthfully.

A few minutes before three about thirty girls in sweaters and caps were waiting on the steps of the gym.

Louise Preston and Florence Guile, eagerly assisted by Lois and Betty, and helpfully, though a little less eagerly by Connie and Angela, were dividing the party into hares and hounds.

"All old girls to the right of the steps, all new girls to the left," ordered Florence. "New girls are hares, old girls, hounds."

"But doesn't some one go with us?" questioned Flora Illington, timidly. She was one of the new girls for whom Mrs. Baird considered a paper chase necessary.

Florence turned to consult Louise, but it was Betty who answered:

"Certainly not," she said decidedly. "You are entirely on your 'own'; choose a leader, and run in any direction."

"But we might get lost," Flora persisted, almost tearfully looking for support to the rest of the hares.

"You can't," Betty assured her; "don't cross any stone walls and you'll be all right. The stone walls are the school boundaries, you can't miss them. Besides, we're sure to find you."

Flora subsided doubtfully, and Louise called:

"Choose your leader."

After a good deal of hesitancy, for the new girls were a little uncertain of one another, Polly Pendleton was selected because she was already generally liked, and partly because she seemed to be thoroughly acquainted with the rules of paper chases.

As Betty gave her the bag of paper she whispered:

"Good luck, and be sure not to go out of bounds."

Polly slung the bag over her shoulder as she answered:

"We won't; how much start do we get?"

"Fifteen minutes," Lois replied, hearing the question and adding, regretfully, "I wish you could go with the hounds."

Just then Louise blew the whistle, and Polly, calling the hares to attention, started off at a dog trot in the direction of the woods.

The hounds, left alone, grouped themselves on the steps to wait until the fifteen minutes were up.

"The trouble with these first races," Connie remarked with a yawn, "is that they are so easy. The hares never know where to go, and we find them a few feet from the pond, and then it's all over. Flora's idea of having an old girl lead them wasn't so bad."

"What! and change a memorable Seddon Hall custom!" exclaimed Angela, jumping to her feet. "Con, I always said you'd no heart, and now I know it. Besides, it's the best thing in the world for the new girls."

"Something tells me, that with Polly Pendleton as a leader they may not be so easy to find this year," Lois mused, gazing along the thin white streak that marked the trail of the hares and disappeared into the depths of the wood beyond.

"Time to start," announced Louise after consulting the gym clock—and the chase began.

An hour later in the heart of the woods, the hounds stopped to consult. Without doubt Lois' prophecy had been fulfilled. The tracking of the hounds had not been easy.

"Where under the sun do you suppose they are?" demanded Betty. "We've been going 'round and 'round in a circle and there's not a sign of them."

"I'll admit I'm completely stumped," said Florence. "This track leads from here to the apple orchard, over the bridge, around to the farm, through the pasture and back to here. Where do we go next?"

"What did I tell you?" asked Lois. "I knew Polly would give us a chase."

"H'm, so did I," Betty agreed, "but I didn't think she'd do it as well as this."

The shadows of the trees lengthening out over the rich black ground gave warning of the approaching sunset.

The hounds looked puzzled.

"Perhaps they have been doubling on the trail, and we've been chasing them around the circle—I say let's go back the way we came, perhaps we'll meet them," suggested Connie.

They all thought this a likely solution, and in a minute they were again in marching order, ready to retrace their steps.

Connie's conjecture was quite true, as far as it went—that was, however, not quite far enough to reach the hares.

Polly, to whom all woods were an open book, once out of sight of the gym, had found her way by various paths to the orchard and, by keeping to the right she discovered the bridge.

"What a piece of luck," she exclaimed to the girls who were running beside her, adding, in explanation:

"If we can only make a circle and come back here, they will never find us—we can stand under the bridge, the brook's almost dry and there are loads of stones."

The other hares, only too eager to be led, acquiesced at once.

Off they started, keeping well to the right, past the farm, and through the pasture, leaving the tiny line of white that later dumbfounded the pursuing hounds. On they sped to the orchard and panting, but delighted, they again reached the bridge.

"Everybody underneath and don't make a sound," Polly warned them, "and keep well to the end so they won't see us as they come along; our only danger is, that they may notice the short trail that leads down here."

They waited for what seemed an age, balancing themselves on slippery stones, very much excited, but very still, save for an occasionally suppressed giggle.

In a few minutes they heard the thump, thump of the approaching hounds and held their breath as the bridge shook over their heads.

"Safe," whispered some one as the sound grew fainter in the distance:

"Where next?"

"Here, of course," replied Polly; "we mustn't move, they are sure to come back."

After the hounds had consulted in the corner of the pasture, they made the circle again. As they reached the bridge for the third time, they were both tired and discouraged. In the middle they halted.

Underneath, the hares huddled breathlessly and Florence Guile's voice came down to them.

"It's after five o'clock, really, I think we'd better give up."

And Betty made answer:

"I suppose so, but it seems dreadful to be beaten by the new girls."

"Hardly by the new girls," laughed Louise, "beaten by that little Polly Pendleton. I don't believe any of the rest could have done it."

So proud were the triumphant hares under the bridge, that they didn't even resent this remark.

"Who can call the loudest?" Louise continued. "Betty, you can tell them we give up, we'll have to go 'round the trail again till we find them."

Betty walked dejectedly to the side of the bridge, pushed her flying hair from her face, put both hands to her mouth and taking a tremendous breath, yelled:

"Come in! Come in! We give up."

Before the echo had died away, sixteen grinning faces appeared from under the bridge.

There was a moment of speechless amazement, and then Polly asked in a quiet voice that contrasted ridiculously with Betty's mighty yell:

"Were you calling us?"

"Look, they're here."

"Under the bridge."

"Where's the trail?"

"Here, look!"

"We're blind!" came the chorus from the startled hounds, followed by:

"How did you do it?"

"Have you been here all the time?"

"Polly, you're a wonder!"

"The new girls never won before."

"Three cheers for Polly!" and suddenly the leader of the hares was the center of an admiring and enthusiastic crowd.

Something had happened, she was no longer just one of the new girls; by this little act, she had won her right to a place in the big school.

Had you asked any of the old girls to explain the difference they would probably have expressed it as Lois had earlier in the day by telling you that:

Polly had proved herself to be thoroughly "Seddon Hallish!"

CHAPTER III—THE WELCOME DANCE TO THE NEW GIRLS

School had opened on Monday and today was Saturday. It had been an exciting week for everybody getting acquainted and settled, and the time had flown.

Today was very important, for it was the date set for the old girls' welcome dance to the new girls. All week there had been whisperings and talk of it, but none of the new girls really knew anything about it.

Friday afternoon the bulletin board had flaunted a poster of a big smiling girl, holding out her arms in welcome to a shy little lass with her finger in her mouth. Mary Williams had painted it, and it was truly a work of art. On it were the words:

WELCOME DANCE TO THE NEW GIRLS
SATURDAY, AT 8 P. M., IN ASSEMBLY HALL

As Polly sat up in bed and stuffed her fingers in her ears—she hadn't grown accustomed to the rising bell yet—she suddenly thought what day it was.

Bouncing out of bed, she slipped into a dressing gown, dashed through the corridor down a flight of stairs to a long room lined on either side with doors leading into tiled bathrooms with sunken porcelain tubs. They had been built only two years, and so magnificent were they after the old ones, that the girls had christened them The Roman Baths and the corridor, Roman Alley.

11

As Polly took the last two steps at a jump, she ran bang into Betty, the freckled face.

"Whither awa' in such mad haste, and what have I ever done to you that you should want to see my poor nose any flatter?" asked Betty, carefully pretending to straighten her nose.

"Oh, I'm so sorry, Betty; did I hurt you?" answered Polly. "I was in such a hurry to get a tub. Some one always beats me, and I've been late to breakfast twice."

"Why not try my stunt and get up ten minutes before the bell? But you're all right this morning," and Betty pointed to the row of open doors. "Turn on the water and then we can talk."

In a minute they were both sitting huddled up on the bottom step, while the water was splashing into their tubs.

"Know who you're going with tonight?" began Betty.

"No. Do you know who has asked me?" inquired Polly.

She had known all week that on the morning of the dance each new girl would receive a written invitation from one of the old girls, asking her to be their guest for the evening.

"Ha, ha," laughed Betty, "don't you wish you knew? Yes, I was there and I heard you bid for; also I was with her when she put the note in your desk. I think you'll be pleased."

"Ah, go on, tell me, please," teased Polly.

"Indeed, I will not," Betty exclaimed. "I will tell you that you won't like Miss Hale any better this time next year than you do now—I will tell you that we will have pancakes for breakfast—or that tomorrow's sermon will be very dull, but tell you the name of the girl who is going to take you tonight, certainly no—"

She stopped short in her dramatic speech as she caught the warning gurgle that water gives in a tub, just a few seconds before it runs over.

"Great Cæsar's Ghost! our baths!" she cried, and both girls dashed for their tubs, and in a minute there came the sound of splashing from behind the closed doors.

Twenty minutes later they met at breakfast, both a little out of breath, and true to Betty's prophecy, there were pancakes.

After breakfast on Saturday there was an hour for study, and after that the girls were free for the rest of the day. Polly could hardly wait to get to her desk, but of course something had to interfere on this particular morning.

Just at the entrance to the schoolroom Miss Hale held out a damp, detaining hand.

"One minute, if you please, Marianna. I want to see you and Angela and Elizabeth" (she meant Betty, of course), "in my room. Your books have come and er—"

Her voice trailed off into a murmur as she sailed down the corridor.

Betty said "The dickens" quite distinctly. Angela looked bored but not rebellious. She shared the other girls' dislike for Miss Hale, but she adored Latin. As for Polly—well, you can fancy how furious she was. There was that note in her desk and Miss Hale might keep them for hours. She wasn't very attentive as the intricacies of Latin grammar were expounded and explained.

However, it did finally end, though not until fifteen minutes after the last study hour bell had rung. Polly, followed by Angela and Betty, started for Study Hall. At the door they ran into a group of girls. Some of them flourished neatly folded notes.

"What are you going to do this morning, Polly?" asked Dot Mead, who was one of the group.

"Come on out for a walk with us," chimed in Helen Reeves and Grace Wright, a long lanky new girl who always agreed with everybody. It may be seen from this that Polly was popular.

"No you don't. She's going with me to watch the basket-ball practice in the gym," Betty interrupted before Polly had a chance to answer.

Just then Angela stepped up and put a note in Polly's hand.

"Forgive my freshness in opening your desk without permission," she said, "but I knew you were crazy to get this, and these wild Indians would have kept you here till luncheon time."

"Angela, you are angelic. Thank you ever so much." And opening the note she read the following:

"Dear Polly:

"Please be my guest at the dance tonight and save me numbers one, three, five, and the last. See you in the corridor after study hour.

"In mad haste,
"Lois."

Polly danced for joy. It was Lois after all, just as she had hoped. She would have been glad, of course, to have gone with Connie or Angela or Betty; she knew them all, perhaps, better than Lois, but then it was easy to know them. It was different with Lois; as often as she had been with her the past week, she felt there was lots left to discover about her.

The extra fifteen minutes that Miss Hale had kept the girls in her room had given Lois time to make her bed, fix her room, and go to the gym. She had left word with Connie, waiting of course, for Angela, to tell Polly where she was.

When the trio reached the corridor, Connie called out:

"Polly, if you're looking for Lois, she's in the gym. She told me to tell you."

And as the girls started for their rooms, she added:

"Don't worry about your beds; I made them."

"You duck," and Betty threw her arms around her neck.

"Yes, you are a duck," agreed Polly. "Thanks awfully."

"Don't be so grateful," called Angela, retiring behind her door for safety. "She only did it so she wouldn't be kept waiting. And they are all probably pied."

"Ungrateful wretch," Connie gasped.

Polly and Betty went after their sweaters, and in a few minutes all four girls were racing for the gym, a low, round building about fifty yards away from the school.

They found Lois, not in a gym suit, as they had expected, but in sweater and cap, evidently waiting for them.

"Hello," she called, "what kept you so long, the Spartan?" (A nickname for Miss Hale.) "Did you get my note?" she continued, turning to Polly.

"Yes, and of course I'm awfully tickled to go with you. You were awfully good to ask me."

Polly's voice was very earnest.

Lois smiled. "Good, that's settled, and now do you want to go into the woods and get some greens with me? Florence Guile and Louise Preston asked me to get some branches for them. They are decorating Assembly Hall and they told me to take another girl with me. We have permission to go out of bounds," she explained.

Then to Betty, who was dramatically tearing her hair:

"Don't look so peevish, Bet, dear, if you expect to make the big team you want to trot on and practice, not wander in the wood."

"Do you know, Lo," Betty answered with a wry smile, "you have the most discouraging habit of telling the truth just when I don't want to hear it. I go. Farewell."

She finished, disappearing through one of the French windows that led into the locker-room.

That long tramp in the woods, on that glorious day, with the fallen leaves almost knee-deep and the crisp wind in their faces, did more to establish the lasting friendship between the two girls than anything else could have done.

Polly, less reticent than Lois, told of her life in the New England town, of the quaint old house, and lingered over the description of her many beloved dogs.

Lois, in turn, described her jolly father, who was a well-known physician, her mother—no one was quite as adorably precious and young as Lois' mother—and her big brother Bob, just seventeen, who was preparing for college.

"You see," she finished, "Dad didn't want me to grow up in a city, and as he has to live in Albany in the winter, he and mother decided I'd better come here."

"I'm awfully glad they did," Polly replied, giving Lois' arm a tight squeeze.

Perhaps the quantity of greens was a little smaller than it might have been, but for these confidences. Still what do greens matter when compared to the forging of a splendid and lasting friendship?

Even confidences must end, and Polly, looking at her wrist watch, a parting gift from Uncle Roddy, exclaimed: "Lois, it's after twelve o'clock. We'll have to fly. I hope you know the way. I'm lost."

They raced back and just had time to scrub their hands and join the end of the luncheon line.

That afternoon they stayed together as a matter of course. They helped the Seniors get the Assembly Hall ready for the dance, and before going to their rooms at dressing hour, they had promised to help serve the ice cream that evening.

Polly was being treated just like an old girl and it seemed hard for her to realize that she had only been at Seddon Hall for one short week.

The dance was a great success, which means no one spoiled it by being homesick, and every one danced all the dances. Ethel Brown and Marjorie Dean almost upset things at the beginning of the fifth dance by getting out handkerchiefs and daubing at their eyes. They were sitting at opposite corners of the room, but didn't think of joining forces.

Lois and Polly, standing near the faculty platform, were just starting their fifth dance when they caught sight of them, and scented danger.

"Look at those two," Lois groaned as she dropped her hand from Polly's shoulder.

Polly looked.

"Bother," she said, "I suppose that means good-bye to our dance."

They parted without hesitation. Lois went over to Ethel and Polly to Marjorie, and as they danced, they listened patiently to a tale of woe, and tried their best to cheer up their self-enforced partners.

After the sixth dance the ice cream and cake and lemonade were served, and for the rest of the evening everything went beautifully. The "good-night bell" rang at ten o'clock, just in the middle of the Virginia reel, but Mrs. Baird, who was on the platform, beckoned to one of the Seniors and gave her permission for it to be finished. When the girls finally did go off to bed, they were all very sleepy and very happy.

As Polly and Lois were leaving the room, Mrs. Baird stopped them.

"Good-night, girls," she said, "you have been a big help to the Seniors, but they have no doubt thanked you for that. I want to tell you that I saw and appreciated your kindness tonight. I am proud of it in you as an old girl," she said to Lois, and then turning to Polly with one of her wonderful smiles that made all the girls adore her, she added:

"And I am more proud to find that same spirit in a new girl."

When Lois and Polly said good-night a few minutes later, Polly whispered:

"Isn't she wonderful?"

"Of course she is," Lois answered, smiling. "I wondered how long it would be before you found it out."

CHAPTER IV—THE CHOOSING OF THE TEAMS

"Polly, there's no use talking, you must learn to play basket-ball."

Lois had delivered this command a couple of days after the paper chase and Polly had therefore spent hours in the gym during the month which elapsed between then and the opening of this chapter.

It was now the first of November. There had already been one or two really cold days, and every one had settled down to the routine of school life. The strangeness had worn off for the new girls, so that they had forgotten they were new.

The chief sport at Seddon Hall was basket-ball. On the first of November every year six girls, from the Junior and Senior classes, were chosen for the big team.

Three days later six substitutes were elected. These twelve girls were the pick of the school, and twice a year they played against an outside team.

Although any girl from any of the four upper classes might be chosen as "subs," the team had hitherto been composed of Juniors and Seniors, with an occasional Sophomore. The captain of the big team was elected early in the term and was always from the Senior class.

Owing to the rather stiff exams of the year before, only eight of the fourteen Juniors had made the Senior class. Those left had not all returned and, counting specials, the Juniors had only eleven girls this year. Fully a third of them were determined to work and had no time for athletics.

There were plenty of Sophomores, fifteen in all, but they were a queer lot. There is always a miscellaneous class and this year it was the "sofs," who had been dubbed "the impossibles."

It had been rumored that on account of the scarcity of girls it was just possible that the team might have to come down to the Freshman class for substitutes, and great was the excitement.

Betty, Polly, and Lois were discussing this unheard-of possibility on their return from practice.

"Of course it is just possible, but—" began Betty.

"No, it's too good to be true," sighed Lois. "Don't let's think about it. But I say those 'sofs' are terrible. Well, I'm going to dress; so long!" And she disappeared into her room.

"Betty, has a Freshman ever been on the sub team before?" Polly inquired.

"Never in my time," answered Betty. "But, then, never, no, never was there such a set of impossibles as the 'sofs,' nor was there ever such a bully center to be found in the Freshman class." This with a meaning glance at Polly, who had managed to get the ball after the toss-up a remarkable number of times that day.

"Bet, you're crazy; why, I'm only a new girl. Lois would be first choice and you second."

"You may be a new girl, but don't forget the paper chase," said Betty. "But you're right about Lo; she is wonderful. She's all over the place at once and she keeps her head. But as for me—no, I haven't a chance."

"Why, Betty, you're splendid at making baskets."

"What good does that do me when I can't keep inside those darn lines? No, it's Lo or you; the rest of us haven't a chance."

16

"Chance for what?" inquired Lois, poking her head out of her room. "Are you two still gabbing? You'll both be late for study hour." And giving each girl a violent push, she brought an end to the conversation.

The choosing of the big team on Tuesday was just about what every one had expected. There were four Seniors and two Juniors; most of them had been substitutes the year before. Louise Preston had already been elected captain.

The list of names had been posted Wednesday morning and the girls had come in for their share of congratulations, but every one felt that the real excitement would come on Friday.

Wednesday, as soon as Miss Hale dismissed them (the Freshmen had Latin the last period, and the Spartan had the most aggravating way of not hearing the bell), Lois, Polly and Betty dashed for the gym.

As they entered, Miss Stuart, the gym teacher, called to them:

"Seven and you three girls make ten. We need two more for a game. Some one go and get Angela and Connie; tell them I think they need some exercise."

Miss Stuart was a large, handsome woman, with a firm but good-natured face. She was renowned for her fairness, and no one had ever even criticized one of her decisions. She had no favorites, and the girls all liked her tremendously.

In a few minutes Betty, who had gone off to search for Angela and Connie, came back, dragging them each by an arm.

"Here they are," she called. "What'll I do with them?"

"Better superintend their getting into their gym suits," answered Miss Stuart, "and make them hurry."

Ten minutes later she blew the whistle and tossed up the ball.

It was a good game. Polly was playing jumping center against Mary Reed, a big heavy girl, slow in her movements, but hard to budge. Connie was playing second center with Polly, and as she was no earthly help, Polly had to bounce the ball to the line and throw it to Betty, who was playing forward. Poor Betty was breaking her record for fouls.

Lois, guarding at the other end, was playing like a little fury. She had to work, for Harriet Ames was so long and lanky that she managed to pick the ball out of the air above her head, unless frantic efforts were used to stop her.

Every one was so busy with the game that the arrival of Louise Preston and two or three members of the big team passed unnoticed. They had slipped in after the game had commenced and were watching each play very carefully.

After the game the three girls met, as usual, in Roman Alley, as the water was running for their cold tubs.

"Hum, I don't call that much of a score—fourteen to four." And Polly sank down on the steps in disgust.

"That's because you were not trying to guard a giraffe with four arms," answered Lois, dropping down beside her.

Betty folded her arms in solemn dignity and stood looking at the two girls on the steps.

"Is it possible, my children," she began, in a voice ridiculously like the school chaplain's, "I repeat, is it possible that you have failed to grasp the full significance of this day's work? Where were your eyes, and have you lost the sense necessary for putting two and two together?"

Polly and Lois looked at her with puzzled expressions.

"Elucidate, Elizabeth, if you please," called a voice from the top of the stairs, accompanied by the click-click of a pair of Chinese slippers. Startled, the girls looked up, half expecting to see Miss Hale descending upon them, but beheld, instead, Angela's grinning face and curly hair above a pale blue woolly wrapper.

"Hey, make room there, you two!" she continued in her own voice, and as she slipped in between Lois and Polly, she added:

"I repeat, elucidate, Elizabeth."

"Lordy," Betty murmured, "what a shock you gave me! The Spartan's had it in for me and I've been trying to dodge her all day. But to continue, you all seem to have lost your share of intelligence. Did you or did you not see Louise Preston and some of the big team girls watching the game? They were writing giddy little lists and having all kinds of solemn powwows with Miss Stuart. Well, the reason is—"

"Stop!" exclaimed Polly. "Betty, you're positively leaping at conclusions. You said yourself no Freshman had ever been chosen."

"And besides," interrupted Lois, "you're making my heart beat twice as fast as it ought to."

"Well, of course," Angela remarked, getting up and stretching, "there's no doubt in my mind that I will be chosen for the sub team. As for the rest of you, you have a chance."

"You!" howled Betty. "A spoofy sub you'd make. You'd be helping Cæsar build his old bridges every time the ball came your way."

Lois looked intently ahead of her.

"Now," she said, "I understand why Bet made all those fouls. Pure flunk, we'd have all done the same thing if we'd known we were being watched. And you never told us—Bet, you're a darling."

"I didn't mean that. I was done for, of course, and I knew it. But pass on the merry news? Certainly not." And Betty, having delivered her pet phrase, made for her bath and slammed the door.

Thursday and Friday mornings passed somehow and the fatal hour arrived. Because of no school on Saturday, the Friday evening study hour was omitted. The time was usually taken up by a lecture or a musical.

There was nothing on for tonight, however, and after dinner the girls collected in the Assembly Hall. Miss Stuart, Louise Preston, and the team were on the platform, and in a few minutes the names of the chosen substitutes were to be read.

Betty, Lois, Polly, Angela, and Connie wandered off together to the farthest corner of the room and tried to look indifferent. Betty shivered.

18

"Shades of the Tower of London," she whispered. "I couldn't feel any creepier if it were the Black List that was going to be read."

"It is uncanny," agreed Connie. "I never miss less than four balls out of every five and yet I feel strangely excited."

Lois and Polly exchanged understanding glances, and then every one began to say hush, and Miss Stuart and Louise stood up on the platform. When everything was quiet, Miss Stuart began:

"Good evening, girls. The captain has asked me to read this list for her. It's the names of the substitutes. If you will answer by coming up to the platform, it will save time and keep the cheering for the end.

`"'First, for guard, Mary Rhine, Junior.`
`Second, for guard, Edith Fisk, Sophomore.`
`Third, for home, Helen Nash, Sophomore.`
`Fourth, for home, Lois Farwell, Freshman.'"`

(And in spite of the gasp of surprise, Miss Stuart continued as if she had said nothing surprising.)

`"'Fifth, for center, Flora Illington, Sophomore.`
`Sixth, for jumping center, Marianna Pendleton,`
`Freshman.'`

"Congratulations, girls, and may—" Miss Stuart's voice was completely drowned in the cheer that went up.

Some one dragged Connie to the piano, and for the rest of the evening they sang school and basket-ball songs and cheered all the six subs in turn.

Of course Polly and Lois were wildly happy, and the entire Freshman class shared in their joy. They boasted of having broken a record and reminded everybody of what might be expected of them when they were lofty Seniors.

It was only when Polly and Lois were alone in their rooms after the "lights out" bell, that they remembered Betty.

Fifteen minutes later, when everything was very quiet along the corridor, two ghost-like figures stole out of two doors and met at a third across the way, and tapped gently.

Betty sat up in bed.

"Who is it?" she whispered.

"It's Polly," answered one ghost.

"It's Lois," answered the other.

A minute later, when they were both curled up on the bed, Lois found Betty's hand and squeezed it.

"Betty, dear, I'm so sorry," she said.

"So am I," agreed Polly. "It's the only disappointment in this glorious day."

"You know you're cut up about it, dear; no use pretending," pursued Lois.

"We saw you leave long before the bell. Oh, Bet—" but Polly was cut short.

19

"Saw me leave? I should think you might have; I didn't leave; I fled. But not because—well not because of what you think, I saw the Spartan coming."

"Then you were not in the 'blues' all evening?" asked Lois doubtingly.

"Certainly not," Betty assured her. "I was studying my Latin, and now do let me go to sleep."

It sounded very well, but as Polly and Lois each gave her a good-night kiss, they noticed a suspicious dampness about her pillow.

They stole safely back to their rooms, conscious of having broken a rule for a good cause and, who knows, perhaps it was because the cause was good that they were not caught.

CHAPTER V—THE THANKSGIVING PARTY

Betty was sitting on top of the grand piano on the platform in the Assembly Hall, kicking her feet and sucking a very large lemon by means of a stick of candy used as a straw.

"Thanksgiving comes but once a year," she chanted to no one in particular, adding, with a heartfelt sigh to give the words emphasis:

"Thank goodness."

"Why so grateful?" questioned Florence Guile pausing in the act of erecting a would-be gypsy tent out of a miscellaneous assortment of shawls. Then, attracted by the gurgling sound of Betty's lemon, she straightened up, and pointing an accusing finger, demanded:

"Betty Thompson, are you daring to suck the lemon we were saving to write the fortunes with?"

"Well, yes I am," Betty admitted, dodging under the piano and smiling impishly from this point of vantage.

"Now, Florence, you are selfish," she teased; "it's bad enough having no Thanksgiving vacation, but after the way I've worked my fingers to the bone for you, you shouldn't, no, you really shouldn't begrudge me a lemon."

Florence tried hard not to smile in the face of Betty's mournful expression, and made an attempt at rescuing the stolen fruit.

The above took place at ten o'clock on Thanksgiving morning. The Assembly Hall was filled with busy girls, and it was evident that preparations of some kind were under way.

Owing to an epidemic of mumps the girls had been kept in school over the holidays, and for their amusement, and to ward off any chance of the more serious epidemic known as "homesickness," the Seniors had been bidden to entertain.

Florence, having unsuccessfully pursued Betty twice around the hall at a rate highly unbecoming a dignified Senior, paused for breath, and Lois, Polly and Angela, who had watched the chase with interest, came to her assistance, and captured the lemon from the now unresisting Betty.

"Here it is, at least what's left of it," said Lois, presenting it to Florence. "And we've finished the spider web in History room. What else can we do for you!"

"Thanks, ever so much," Florence replied. "That settles the little children, they will be in there by themselves. Now if you'll only struggle with that tent, I can't make it look like anything."

"Don't worry about it, I think I can," Lois assured her, "it's for the gypsies to sit in and tell the fortunes, isn't it!"

"Yes, but it will never be large enough," Florence responded dolefully.

"Well, let them sit at the door of it," suggested Angela; "that will be just as picturesque and not nearly so hot."

Florence looked with admiration at the girls before her.

"What wonders you are," she said. "You've done all the work so far, it's lots more the Freshmen's party than the Seniors'."

"But you and Louise can't be expected to do it all," replied Polly, decidedly. "And you know you're the only two that count," she added, lowering her voice so that the other Seniors, who were willingly, but unsuccessfully, attempting the decorations at the other end of the room, would not hear her.

Florence, a little confused at such frank praise, said hurriedly:

"Well, you're dears to do it anyway and now, if you'll do something with that tent I'll fly to Louise. I promised to help her with those fortunes. We have to write one for every girl, and it will take ages."

"Poor dear, and to think I sucked up half the lemon," said Betty contritely. "I'll go get you some milk, it's just as good," she finished, starting for the door.

"You can't," Angela called after her. "The storeroom's closed."

Betty, already out of the room, whirled around on one toe, and holding to the side of the doorway for support, poked her laughing face around the corner.

"Then, I'll steal it from the cat," she said.

For the rest of the morning, Angela and Polly, under the able directions of Lois, who was undoubtedly very artistic, worked over the tent and succeeded in making it look quite habitable.

"It's not perfect but I guess it will do. I wish we could get a big kettle," Lois said, as she stood off with her head on one side to get the effect.

"Well, can't we," questioned Polly. "There's sure to be one in the kitchen."

Angela, who was busy with the finishing touches, remarked hopefully:

"The lights will be dim tonight and that ought to help."

Lois walked to the edge of the platform and asked some of the Seniors who were still busy at the other end of the room, to come and see if the tent was all right.

After they had eyed it critically, and suggested one or two unimportant changes—thereby asserting their superiority—they pronounced it perfect. The three girls sat down for a well merited rest.

In the mean time, Florence and Louise, in the latter's room, were racking their brains over the fortunes.

Before the lemon was used up, Betty appeared with a half a glass of milk, but she absolutely refused to tell where she had found it.

"Well, it doesn't much matter anyway, as long as it wasn't the cat's," Louise laughed, giving up trying to discover. "But now that you're here you may as well stay and help us with these things."

"My massive brain is at your service," Betty replied, flopping on the bed, and preparing to make herself thoroughly comfortable.

"Haven't you done any of them yet?"

"Dozens," answered Florence, "like 'you will grow wise and wax fat' that will do for anybody, but some of the girls must have special ones."

"Who are they?"

"First, there's Mary Reeves."

"Oh! say she'll make the team her first year in college," suggested Louise. "Who next?"

"Madelaine Ames, what about her?"

Louise looked puzzled.

"The professors refused to teach her music any more," said Betty, doubtfully. "Says she's incorrigible—like that, through his nose."

"Good, we'll say she will go on a concert tour, and take the world by storm. Now who?"

"Well, there's Agnes Green," Louise hesitated.

Agnes was one of the Seniors, with little or no popularity; a girl, lacking the essentials of a leader, and yet always refusing to conform or follow. Seddon Hall called her a grouch, and passed her by.

"Ugh! I hate her," exclaimed Betty; "leave her out."

The two older girls exchanged glances. They agreed heartily, but loyalty to their class-mate kept them silent.

"We can't, she's a Senior," Louise said quietly.

"Well then, condemn her to a horrible end with my love," Betty replied.

Florence ruffled her hair and looked thoughtful.

"She's rather fond of the boys," she said. "We might say that she will be the first in the class to marry."

"Weak," Louise criticized, "but it will do. Now who?"

"Luncheon, by the sound of that," laughed Florence as the big gong sounded in the lower hall.

"We'll have to finish these later—come on." And after a hasty dab at their hair, they hurried out to join the line.

Thanksgiving dinner was a very jolly affair. Each table was decorated with flowers and fruit, and each had a turkey to itself.

Mrs. Baird had her soup with the Seniors; her turkey with the Juniors; her salad with the Sophomores; her dessert with the Freshmen; and her coffee and nuts with the faculty.

It was noticeable that each table enjoyed itself the most and laughed the heartiest during the course that she ate with them.

The afternoon passed quickly, and by six o'clock the girls and faculty were all tramping into the Assembly Hall, that in the dim shaded light resembled a wooded dell, fit background for the gypsy camp that occupied one end of it.

Supper consisted of chicken salad, all kinds of sandwiches, cake, lemonade and ice cream. Just the sorts of things it's fun to eat, sitting on the floor, picnic fashion.

In spite of the big dinner, every one ate heartily.

By eight o'clock the musical program was over. Edith Thornton's little Irish Songs received their well merited applause. Two or three amusing recitations were given and then the fortune telling began.

The younger children were sent into the History room to entangle the spider web of every color twine that wound in and out all over the room. Every child was given her end of her color string, and they at once set out to discover the prize hidden somewhere, and tied firmly to the other end.

In the big room, some of the lights were put out and the girls sat in hushed groups talking in whispers.

Every once in a while, a Senior dressed as a gypsy would single out a group and lead it to the camp, where Louise and Florence as fortune tellers would select their fortunes from a big black pot (Polly's discovery) and read it out in a sing-song voice. If it was one of the special ones, it would be received with peals of laughter from the listening girls.

Angela, Connie, Lois, Betty and Polly sat in a circle in one corner of the room. They completely surrounded and hid from view what had been the choicest plate of cakes.

Polly looked with admiration at Betty as she finished her seventh piece.

"Bet, dear," she asked, "how do you manage to eat so much. The rest of us are birdlike beside you."

"I concentrate," was the reply, "it's really very simple."

"Will some one kindly divert her attention elsewhere for a while then," Angela requested, "for there's only one piece left and I mean to have it."

The others, as soon as they too perceived this lamentable fact, made a frantic dive for the dish, but just who would have carried off the prize will never be known, for at that moment, one of the gypsies, catching sight of the group, called to them:

"You're wanted on the platform. They are waiting to tell your fortunes, hurry up."

Scrambling to their feet, the girls followed their guide to the tent and waited.

Very slowly Louise stirred the contents of the black pot, and silence fell upon the room as she held up an apparently plain sheet of white paper.

"Betty Thompson," she chanted, and after holding the slip over a candle until the words written in milk appeared brown and mysterious, she read:

"You will become a famous Latin scholar, but you will die an early death from indigestion."

23

Roars of laughter greeted this prophecy, for all knew how Betty hated Latin. Florence Guile read the next.

"Connie Wentworth," she droned, "you will make a world wide reputation as an actress, starring first as Lady Macbeth."

The old girls understanding the allusion to Connie's escapade of the year before were delighted. Then came Angela's fortune and Louise read it with a smile.

"Upon reaching your second childhood, at the age of eighty-two, you will begin a strenuous and athletic life. Basket-ball and paper chases will be your chief joy."

"What a doom," groaned Angela, as she staggered from the platform amid hearty cheers.

Florence nearly burned up Lois' fortune which came next, and had some difficulty in reading it.

"You will achieve success as a great artist and excel in stage settings. You will have one friend of whom you will never tire," she finally announced.

"I engage you at once," cried Connie, when the laughter subsided. "You can design all the scenes for my plays."

"That's easy," Lois retorted. "All you need is a staircase, a nightgown and a daub of red paint."

"Polly Pendleton," announced Louise, and the girls stopped talking at once, "you will become a Joan d'Arc and plan successful marches for many armies, after having been selected captain of basket-ball in your Senior year and leading the team to brilliant victories."

"Mercy! all of that?" gasped Polly, half laughing, half serious.

The girls clapped and cheered her until Mrs. Baird mounted the platform.

"I think," she said, "this has been a splendid Thanksgiving. I'm sure we're all very grateful to the Seniors. I can't say I wish all the fortunes to come true, for that would be a calamity, but I hope the nice ones will, and now, good-night."

The party was over, and the girls swarmed through the door laughing and talking.

Polly and Lois found themselves alone in the Assembly Hall. It looked strangely bedraggled and lonely, like a starched party dress after the party.

They started for their rooms together—Lois said:

"Well, it's all over, but wasn't it fun?"

"Rather, the fortunes were great."

"Yours was the best of all."

"Yours is more likely to come true."

"They both might."

They separated at Polly's door and entered their own rooms.

Among the many things that filled their thoughts, the fortunes were soon forgotten. They did not know that at a future date, Polly, after three splendid years at Seddon Hall, and Lois, after a longer time, would look back with amusement tinged with wonder, at the truth of those same fortunes.

CHAPTER VI—A RAINY DAY

"Finished your outline, Betty?" Lois called out as the girls were leaving the schoolroom after the last bell one afternoon.

"Certainly not," answered Betty excitedly. "I started to read just the first scene, but when I got to 'By my troth, Nerissa, my little body is a-weary of this great world,' at the beginning of the second scene, why I just read on all the last period."

It was the first lesson of the Freshman class on "The Merchant of Venice." They had finished Goldsmith's "Deserted Village," and this was their first taste of Shakespeare.

"Hadn't you read it before?" questioned Polly. "I have, and I adore it."

"Adore what?"

It was Lois speaking, of course. She had a habit of coming up unexpectedly and hearing the last couple of words of a sentence.

"The Merchant of Venice," explained Polly. "Have you started it?"

"Yes. I read it, the last two periods. I'm as far as 'My Daughter! O my ducats!' I nearly died laughing over Launcelot Gobbo."

It was a miserable day; the sun seemed to have abdicated in favor of his brother, the storm cloud, and the rain was falling in torrents. Betty turned disconsolately towards the window. They were standing in the schoolroom corridor.

"Looks as if we were in for another deluge," she groaned. "Not even a chance of a let-up. Now, if it would only freeze!"

"What can we do?" sighed Lois. "Assembly Hall will be mobbed by the lower school girls, and you know the noise they make."

"I have it!" exclaimed Polly. "Let's get permission from Miss Porter to use the English room, and then each take parts and read 'The Merchant of Venice' aloud."

"Polly, you're a genius; it's the very thing," chorused Lois and Betty.

They started off in the direction of the classroom, but as they passed the Bridge of Sighs, they were stopped by the two Dorothys.

"Where are you going? Come on up to the corridor. Miss King has lent us the electric stove from the infirmary, and we're going to make candy," they invited.

"It's quite regular," added Dot Mead, by way of explanation. "We have permission."

Dot had often tried to inveigle the three girls into joining various midnight feasts and forbidden larks of which she was the originator, but had always found them singularly unresponsive.

Don't think they were prudes, far from it, but they had learned through close observation that not enough pleasure could be derived from breaking rules to compensate them for the loss of the faculty's respect and trust. And, above all, their loyalty and love for Seddon Hall prompted them to keep the few simple rules required of them.

Betty regarded the two girls with lofty disdain and assuming an attitude peculiar to the long-suffering chaplain, began in imitation of his manner:

"There would seem a certain amount of er—er—one might say—attractiveness in your suggestion to an outsider, Dorothy, my child, one, let us say, not familiar with your ability as a cook. For me, however, the invitation holds no charms. Last time, if you'll remember, you put hair oil in the taffy in place of the vanilla. I need hardly refer to the disastrous results." And clasping her hands behind her back, the wicked little mimic walked off down the corridor, adding over her shoulder: "Good afternoon, my dear young ladies, good afternoon."

By this time the girls were holding their sides with laughter. Finally Dorothy managed to ask very weakly:

"Then what are you going to do?"

"There's not the slightest use in telling you, for you'd never believe it," Polly answered. "Still, as you've asked, I'll tell you. We are going to study."

This startling announcement was too much for the Dorothys, and when Lois and Polly left them, to follow Betty, they were lying in mock faints on the corridor floor.

The three girls proceeded to English room and knocked gently on the door.

"Come in," called Miss Porter's voice from the other side.

She was a short, dark, little lady, with glowing black eyes and unlimited enthusiasm. She was very bashful out of the classroom and the girls, as a whole, knew very little of her. Just now she was correcting Senior papers and was a little surprised at being interrupted.

As the three girls entered the room Lois, ever the spokesman in serious matters, began:

"Oh, are we disturbing you, Miss Porter? We didn't think you'd be busy and we wanted permission to sit in here and read 'The Merchant of Venice' aloud."

"You see," added Polly, "we thought it would be fun for each to take parts and—and—" she was floundering for words.

"And act it," finished Miss Porter. "Do you really like it, girls? I am so glad. Sit down, of course." Then regretfully: "I'll be finished in a minute."

Betty caught the regret in her voice and exclaimed impulsively:

"Won't you stay? It would be so much nicer; you can't have anything to do on this miserable day."

Lois and Polly added their pleas to hers and in the end Miss Porter remained.

They decided that Lois take the part of *Portia* and *Jessica*; Polly, *Nerissa* and *Bassanio*; Betty, *Antonio*, *Gratiano*, and *Lorenzo*, and they all insisted on Miss Porter being *Shylock*. They took turns with the smaller parts.

They had rather improvised stage property, but they managed to get on somehow until they reached the casket scene.

"Now what under the sun are we going to use for the caskets?" demanded Betty.

"We might use the 'Standard Dictionary' for the lead one," suggested Miss Porter; "and here's the 'Cyclopedia of Names'—that might do for the silver one."

"I've found the very thing for the gold casket," announced Lois, who was standing in front of the bookcase: "A complete set of Shakespeare in one volume."

"The very thing," they agreed.

The stage setting was arranged and the play continued. Betty constituted herself the musician and sang: "Tell me where is fancy bred, etc.," to a tune all her own.

An hour passed and they started the fourth act.

"I don't feel a bit like a judge," announced Lois, "and, Miss Porter, you ought to have a beard, but never mind. Let's see; this is the court room and—"

"The judge ought to sit in a prominent place," interrupted Betty. "I know—a chair up there." And she swung a light cane visitor's chair on the English room's dignified and highly polished oak desk.

The stage ready, the scene began. *Bassanio* pleaded with *Shylock* for *Antonio's* life, but *Shylock* gloatingly demanded his pound of flesh. *Portia*, as the learned judge, made answer.

"A pound of that same merchant's flesh is thine: The Court awards it, and the law doth give it."

Shylock rubbed his hands together joyously and gurgled: "Most rightful judge!"

Portia: "And you must cut this flesh from off his breast: The law allows it, and the court awards it."

Shylock: "Most learned judge! A sentence! Come, prepare!"

Then Lois rose and, holding up a warning arm, began with suppressed excitement, while they all watched her, intent on the coming speech.

Portia:

"Tarry a little; there is something else!
This bond doth give thee here no jot of blood,—
The words expressly are, a pound of flesh:
Take then thy bond, take thou thy pound of—"

"Candy," called a voice from the hall, and in a second the door opened and Uncle Roddy, preceded by Mrs. Baird, entered.

Lois nearly toppled off the desk in her surprise and Miss Porter, who had fallen, groveling on the floor, at the words "no jot of blood," scrambled to her feet with a very red face.

"Uncle Roddy!" exclaimed Polly, "where did you come from?" And she threw her arms around his neck.

27

"From Buffalo, my dear," answered Uncle Roddy. "I found I could stop over here for a couple of hours on my way home. I am so glad I did, for I wouldn't have missed this for the world. Please introduce me to the rest of the company."

Mrs. Baird made the introductions and then turned to leave them. Before she closed the door she said:

"Girls, if you have been at this all the afternoon, I think you might be excused from study hour." Then to Polly she added: "I'll send tea to the reception-room at once."

Of course Uncle Roddy insisted on "the companies" joining them for tea. Miss Porter had to decline the invitation on account of a special class at 4:30, but Betty and Lois accepted with pleasure.

After they were comfortably settled in the reception-room, Uncle Roddy asked:

"Miss Farwell, are you, by any chance, related to Doctor Walter Farwell?"

"I should think so," laughed Lois. "I'm his daughter. Do you know him?"

"I used to go to college with him. We were great pals, then, but after we graduated he went West and I went to England, and we lost track of each other."

"I'll write him about you this very night," answered Lois excitedly. "Isn't it fun to think you know each other?"

Uncle Roddy smiled. "I'd like to see old Walter again," he said.

The tea arrived and Polly served. Every one did justice to it and the hot buttered toast.

"How long had you and Mrs. Baird been listening at the door, Mr. Pendleton?" inquired Betty as she dropped four lumps of sugar into her cup.

"Long enough to feel sure that you will make a very great actress one of these days," laughed Uncle Roddy.

"Actress!" she exclaimed, taken by surprise. "Certainly not! I intend to write."

The secret was out and Betty, who had never intended telling any one her one great wish, was terribly confused.

Uncle Roddy, however, was deeply interested, and he talked books with her for the rest of his visit. He was greatly surprised that any one so young should have read and appreciated so much.

Polly and Lois joined in the conversation every now and then, but contented themselves most of the time with the candy that Uncle Roddy had brought, which, by the way, was five pounds instead of one.

When his time was up, the three girls escorted him to the door.

"I've had a splendid time," he told them. "I'll surely send you that book," he added to Betty, and then turning to Lois he called: "Don't forget to give my regards to your father."

After a last kiss and hug for Polly, he closed the front door, and the girls watched him jump into his cab.

"Do you know, Polly," announced Betty, as they returned to the corridor, "I adore that uncle of yours."

"So do I," agreed Lois; "he's a duck, and I'm so glad he and Dad know each other."

Polly smiled happily.

"Funny thing," she replied, "but do you know, so do I."

As the carriage jogged through the mud on its way to the station, Uncle Roddy decided that visiting and having tea with three very interesting and lively young ladies was much more entertaining then he had expected.

CHAPTER VII—BETTY'S DUCKING

Betty was bored. The impatient look in her eyes and the disgusted expression of her mouth could be described by no other word.

She leaned dejectedly against a big tree on the edge of the pond and watched the girls skate round and round in dizzy circles. A white boy's sweater enveloped her slender body and accentuated the forlorn droop of her shoulders. Her white berry cap was pulled rakishly over one ear.

There was nothing apparently in the scene before her to warrant dissatisfaction. The sky showed a cloudless front, the sun was shining with determined cheerfulness over the snow-covered grounds, and the pond was frozen over with smooth mirror-like ice that beckoned invitingly to the most exacting skater.

Her wish of the previous chapter, that the rain would freeze, was certainly fulfilled.

Besides, it was Saturday morning, study hour was over, and the rest of the glorious day was free, yet, despite all these blessings, Betty was bored.

Polly and Lois, who were among the laughing group of girls on the ice, separated themselves from the rest and skated over to her.

"What's the matter, Bet, why aren't you skating?" questioned Lois.

Betty pulled off a strip of bark from the tree, broke it up into little pieces and threw them one by one into the pond.

"What's the use?" she answered. "I'm sick to death of going round and round and round again on this silly pond, stumbling every minute over some girl that doesn't know how to skate."

Polly and Lois exchanged glances.

"Why, Betty, you're positively peevish; what side of the bed did you get out of?" Polly laughed.

"Perhaps I am; anyhow, I'm sick of this. Why can't we skate on the river where there's more room?"

"I suppose we could, if we got enough girls together, found a chaperone and got permission," said Lois slowly.

"Oh! but wouldn't that be wonderful!" Polly exclaimed, "let's do it."

Betty brightened up, and looked a little more cheerful at the prospect of a lark.

"Who'll we get to go?" she demanded, now thoroughly alive.

"Angela and Connie."

"They can't skate well enough."

"Never mind, let's ask them."

"Oh, all right, who else?"

"We don't want too many."

"How about Louise?"

"And Florence?"

"Of course, if they'll come."

"That makes seven."

"Isn't that enough?"

"Who for chaperone?"

"Miss Stuart."

"She's sick."

"Miss King then."

"The Infirmary's full, she wouldn't be able to."

"Miss Porter?"

"She's gone to New York with the other teachers, to the opera."

"I forgot, who's left?"

"The Spartan."

"Never!" objected Betty strenuously, "it can't be—why, we'd no sooner get to the river than her feet would be cold, or her nose or her hands, and we'd have to turn back; besides, she doesn't skate."

"All the better," Lois said; "we can build her a nice little fire and make her quite comfy on shore, out of the breeze, and then leave her."

"Now, Bet, don't be so particular, she's our only hope," reminded Polly.

After a good deal of persuasive arguing, Betty finally consented, and they started off to ask the other girls.

They found Angela and Connie coasting on the big hill.

"Wait a second, you two," Betty called to them.

They pulled their sleds off the track into a snow bank and came over to her.

"What do you want?" asked Connie; "isn't the coasting great?"

"Yes, but the skating is better," said Lois, "specially on the river."

"Elucidate," said Angela.

Polly began:

"Well, it's this way," she explained; "Betty's in a fearful mood, the worst possible stage of grouch, nothing suits her. The pond's too small, and she objects to the girls who don't know how to skate as well as she does; she says they're in her way. Well, there's nothing for her but to walk it off. We thought a select, mind, a very select number of girls and a chaperone, and an afternoon on the river, where she'd have plenty of room, might soothe her. Will you and Connie come?"

"With the solemn understanding that if you crack the whip, I don't have to be end man," answered Connie, thinking of the many times she had been sent spinning across the ice.

"I'll go because it's a select party," laughed Angela. "And because I'm tired of this hill. Who else is going?"

"We thought we'd ask Louise and Florence, and perhaps they'll want some of the other Seniors; we had to have some old girls along and they're the nicest," Betty told her.

"Have you got permission?"

"Not yet."

"Who's going to chaperone?"

"The Spartan."

"You're joking."

"We are not."

"But—"

"She's the only one left, the rest of the faculty are in New York, or busy."

"Who's to ask her?"

It was Angela who asked the question, and Lois pointing at her answered: "You."

"Never!"

"You must!"

"But why?"

"Because you are the only one who has recited intelligently in class for the past week."

Angela gasped in astonishment tinged with amusement.

"It's a plot," she announced tragically, "and I'm the victim. Oh, very well, I'll do it," she ended stoically as if the deed in view was one of awful villainy.

"Be very polite to her," cautioned Polly. "Tell her we want her very much, and don't let her say no. Bet, you have to ask Mrs. Baird."

"Oh, make Lois."

"No, you have to, Lo and I are going to ask Louise and Florence."

"I like that—"

"Come on, we must hurry," Lois interrupted her, catching Polly's arm and starting for the house.

Angela followed holding tightly to Connie, who she insisted had to come with her to back her up.

"I'll meet you in your room, Lo," Betty called over her shoulder as she parted from the rest under the Bridge of Sighs, on her way to Mrs. Baird's office.

Polly and Lois left Angela and Connie waiting to learn if the permission were granted before venturing to ask the Spartan, and hurried on to Senior Alley.

They found Louise and Florence in the latter's room, studying.

They were delighted with the idea when Polly explained it to them, said they didn't care to include any of the other Seniors, and stopped work to go up to Lois' room and wait for Betty. They had been there only a few minutes when she burst in upon them.

"It's all right, we can go," she announced delightedly. "Mrs. Baird was adorable about it, she suggested that we take a couple of the older girls, and I told her we were going to ask Louise and Florence. She said that was good, and she smiled; I know she wanted to laugh when I told her we were going to ask the Spartan to chaperone."

This was true; Betty's face had been so cast down when she explained that Miss Hale was the only available teacher, that Mrs. Baird, who understood girls as few women can, had difficulty in suppressing a smile.

At that moment Angela and Connie entered the room.

"She won't go," they announced in unison, "says she feels a cold coming on."

"I knew it!"

"That's too mean."

"There's not another teacher left."

"What'll we do?"

"Leave it to me," Louise said slowly. "I think I can fix it, I'll go talk to her. Wait here for me." And she was gone.

The girls waited, carrying on a fragmentary conversation, and in less than fifteen minutes Louise returned. She was met by a volley of questions:

"Will she go?"

"What did she say?"

"Tell us the worst."

"How did you fix it?"

She put both fingers in her ears in protest.

"Stop talking so much and I'll tell you," she said. "Miss Hale is not going, but Mrs. Baird is."

"No!"

"Really!"

"She's a darling."

"What a lark."

The girls were overcome with surprise and delight.

Lois managed to say a whole sentence without being interrupted.

"Louise, you're a wonder, how did you ever manage it!"

"I explained about Miss Hale's cold and asked her if she could think of any one else. She suggested going herself and of course I wouldn't leave until I'd made her promise that she would."

"Does she skate?" inquired Angela.

"She used to, but she said she didn't think she would today. She's going to take a book along."

"We'll build her a fire," said Lois.

"Out of the wind," added Polly.

"Let's take a steamer rug," Betty said, not to be outdone, and the rest added other suggestions.

The plans that had been offered earlier in the morning for the utter obliteration of the Spartan were now converted into plans for the ease and comfort of Mrs. Baird.

At three o'clock every one was ready to start, the girls armed with skates and hockey sticks. Mrs. Baird, dressed in a rough tweed walking suit, carried a book, and looked, save for her gray hair, as young as either of the Seniors.

"Come along," she called, "we've a long walk ahead of us and time is flying." And off they started.

The steep descent that led to the river from Seddon Hall proved to be, not only long, but very tedious. The path was completely hidden by the snow, and an unseen tree root or stone caused many a trip up that terminated in a long slide down hill.

It was so funny to see some one suddenly plunge up to their waist in deep snow, and then roll, arms and legs in the air, for five or ten feet, that the girls were in hysterics most of the walk.

When the river was finally reached without mishap and too much loss of time, they were weak from laughing.

"Well," announced Mrs. Baird, tears of mirth in her eyes; she had had her share of troubles too, "we will not go back that way, we would never reach home. We'll go through the village by way of the station. Now don't bother about me, get on your skates," she added, as she saw the girls spreading out a steamer rug and collecting bits of wood for a fire.

But they insisted on making her comfortable first.

Polly and Betty made a fire and Louise and Florence fixed the rug in a small enclosure made by a clump of bushes, and situated directly under a big overhanging rock.

When these preparations were over, Mrs. Baird settled down comfortably and opened her book, and the girls put on their skates.

"Say what you please," said Polly, "it's not as smooth here as it was on the pond, and there's a crack over there."

This was true. The sun had been shining steadily, and in spots the ice had melted on the river, leaving an inch or so of slush on the surface.

"Never mind, we can keep away from it, we've the whole place to ourselves," exulted Betty, looking out over the expanse of ice, and not seeing a single person in sight. "Come on!"

Off they glided each by herself, at first, to get the swing. Then they organized a hockey game, and for a while they skated furiously.

"Fifth time for you, Bet, you're a wonder," Florence called as Betty sent the flat disc sailing past Angela, through the goal posts that were serving in place of cages.

33

"Oh! I can't stop those, they come too fast; somebody change places with me," said Angela. "This is too strenuous for me."

"Oh, nonsense," cried Polly. "Get in the game, Ange, come on up in the center, I'll play guard, if you like."

"All right."

"Everybody ready?"

"Play."

"Zip," sang the puck, darting here and there, in obedience to the click, click of the busy hockey sticks.

Florence and Lois were fighting over it. Polly, Betty, Connie and Louise tried to interfere, and for a minute there was a wild skirmish. In the excitement, Angela, who was hovering around the outside, got in some one's way and fell flat.

"Stop, Ange is down."

"What did you do that for?" Angela demanded, as she sat up and rubbed her back. "I thought I was keeping out of it."

"Did you hurt yourself?"

"No, not much, but I've had enough."

"So have I."

"What will we do next?"

"Let's crack the whip," suggested Betty. "You lead, Con."

"Not I, I can't go fast enough."

"Louise, you lead."

"All right, who's on the end."

Lois opened her mouth to speak and stopped. She was looking over Louise's shoulder. Coming toward her were four boys dressed in the uniform of the Military School that was situated on another hill along the Hudson, about five miles north of Seddon Hall. She knew who they were at once, for she had often passed groups of them in the village, or met them when out on a straw ride.

"Look," she said in an undertone, for the boys were already within ear shot.

The girls turned.

"Oh! the dickens," exclaimed Betty crossly, "why couldn't they have gone somewhere else?"

Mrs. Baird had also seen the new arrivals and noticed the girls' hesitation. She beckoned Louise to her side.

"Don't pay any attention to them," she said, "and I'm sure they won't disturb you."

Louise nodded and returned to the girls.

"Let's play hockey again," she suggested.

"What about the boys?" inquired Connie.

"Don't pay any attention to them."

"Well, come on, let's start," Florence whirled into position. But Angela's eyes were glued to the group of boys.

"Stop staring," Betty whispered.

"I can't help it, I never saw a boy with redder hair." Instinctively they all turned.

"Carrots."

"Brick top."

"Stop, this is terrible, let's start something."

"All right, get ready."

"Go!"

They took their positions and were again skirmishing after the puck.

"Oh, let's quit, I'm dead," Angela pleaded weakly, after they had played for a time. She had been buffeted about until she was completely winded.

"All right, lazy, you rest and we'll crack the whip," teased Betty.

As she said it, she took a chance whack at the puck with her hockey stick and sent it spinning. Over the ice it flew, while the girls looked on in fascinated horror, for it was heading directly for the boys, and never stopped until it had landed at the feet of the red-headed one.

"Betty!" gasped Lois.

Angela giggled outright. Then, for almost a minute there was absolute silence. All eyes were centered on the puck.

At last the red-headed boy lifted his stick and sent it back.

Betty called "Thank you ever so much," and he answered:

"Don't mention it," and pulled off his military cap, completely uncovering his fiery head. Then he and his friends skated off in the opposite direction.

"It is red, and no mistake," laughed Florence.

"It's a wonder it doesn't melt the ice," Angela answered. "What's the matter, Bet?" she added.

"You're all very unkind, he can't help it," Betty replied, straightening up. "I'm sure he's most polite. I like him," she finished decidedly.

The girls didn't know whether to tease her or not, so, to change the subject, Louise suggested the forgotten game.

"Get ready for crack the whip," she said. "Bet, you lead."

"All right, get ready—"

"Who's on the end!"

"Polly."

"Go ahead—"

The girls put their hands on one another's shoulders, forming a long line, and Betty started off, skating fast and keeping straight ahead. Suddenly, when everybody was going like the wind she gave a sharp turn to the right and the girls went pell mell in every direction.

It was loads of fun and very invigorating. They played it over and over again, each girl taking a turn to lead.

"Polly's first this time," called Louise, "and Betty's last."

"Be merciful, Poll," Betty panted, taking hold of Lois' shoulders.

"I will not," laughed Polly. "Get ready—Go!"

Off they started for perhaps the sixth time. They were now well out from shore, and in places the ice was quite slushy. Polly raced ahead, never giving a thought about anything but the joy of sailing along with the wind in her face.

As she made the quick turn, the ice under their feet gave a sickening longdrawn "whirr-r" followed by a sharp crack.

For a minute there was pandemonium—what followed came very much more swiftly than it can be told.

There was a wild dash for firm ice—a startled scream and then the horrible picture of Betty struggling, and up to her neck in the water.

Lois and Polly made frantic efforts to reach her, but at every attempt the ice gave another warning crack.

Mrs. Baird, on the shore, called desperately for help, and the other girls stood rigid with fear.

It seemed an eternity, and then, the red-headed boy came, quickly, purposefully, and took command. He sent his friends for ropes and boards, while he himself lay down flat on the ice and wormed his way towards Betty.

She was still keeping up. Luckily the hole was small and she was wedged in between two big chunks of ice.

Lois and Polly stood helpless, waiting. Finally he called to them: "Get the rest and form a chain to me. Some one catch hold of my feet—Easy now."

The girls obeyed quickly and he crawled along until he could touch Betty. Very skillfully he took hold of her under her arms.

"Don't struggle," he warned her. "You're all right." And mustering every bit of his strength, he pulled her gently on to the ice beside him. "Now pull me back," he ordered.

When his friends returned with the rope, she was safe on shore rolled up in the steamer rug, and Mrs. Baird was beside her. He was the center of an admiring and relieved crowd of girls, who were all talking at once.

Still master of the occasion he dispatched one of his friends for a carriage, and another for a warm drink. "And," he added severely, after he had given them their directions, "don't be so blame long about it this time."

The warm drink arrived first—it was in a flask—and Mrs. Baird administered it sparingly.

Then the carriage arrived and she left Betty and came over to the others.

"You have been splendid," she said to the red-headed boy. "I have no words in which to thank you. I shudder to think what we would have done without you." She pressed his hand gratefully. "Thank you," she repeated, with a hint of tears in her voice.

36

The red-headed boy, though a hero, was easily embarrassed.

"Oh, please," he stammered, "it was all right. Nothing at all. Here, let me help you get her in the carriage," he added hastily, glad of anything that would put a stop to these embarrassing thanks, and because he wanted one more look at Betty.

This wish was of course mere curiosity. If a chap saves a girl's life, surely he had the right to know what she looked like, or so he argued with himself.

"Thank you, if you will," Mrs. Baird replied.

And together they lifted Betty into the back of the carriage. The steamer rug enveloped her like a mummy cloth, but as they got her safely on the seat, one corner of it fell away, and revealed to the red-headed boy her white face and blue lips, that tried so bravely to smile up into his eyes.

The carriage jogged off at a snail's pace—Mrs. Baird knelt on the floor beside Betty, the girls walked along the road easily keeping up with it.

The red-headed boy watched the queer procession; he still held his hat in his hand, and his flaming hair was the last thing the girls saw.

Hours later, safe in the infirmary, surrounded by hot water bottles and woolly blankets, Betty opened her eyes—she had been asleep—and encountered those of Mrs. Baird.

"What was his name?" she asked drowsily.

"My darling child, I forgot to ask him!" exclaimed Mrs. Baird; "how very remiss of me."

Betty's gaze wandered around the room, then her eyes closed again.

"Doesn't matter," she said slowly. "He'd always have been just the red-headed boy to me."

CHAPTER VIII—CUTTING THE LECTURE

Polly awoke with a start and bounded out of bed as the rising bell clanged down the corridor.

"I knew it, I knew it; my Latin won't be finished and the Spartan will be furious," she exclaimed to the four walls, "but I did intend to get up early. Well, it can't be helped now; hateful stuff, anyhow."

For two days the snow had been falling, and the coasting had been perfect. As might be expected, lessons had suffered. The girls would come into study hours flushed with excitement, their blood tingling and their eyes sparkling, and it was only the most studious that could get down to real concentrated work.

It was Friday morning, and a particularly glorious day. The grounds were covered with snow three feet deep, the main hill where the girls coasted had been shoveled out, stamped down, and refrozen until it resembled a broad ribbon of ice with high banks of drifted snow on either side.

The fir trees were weighed down to the ground, icicles hung from the porches of the school building, and the gym looked like an ice palace.

This enticing scene, with sunshine over all, made Polly look longingly from the corridor window on her way to Latin class, a couple of hours after we left her thinking of her unprepared lesson.

"I wish it were the last period instead of the first," Lois whispered, catching up with her and linking her arm in hers.

"So do I, for a lot of reasons," groaned Polly. "In the first place, I haven't my Latin finished, and in the second, well, it's a crime to stay indoors on a day like this."

"Really, girls, I must remind you, there is no talking allowed in the corridors."

The Spartan was upon them. One never heard her coming; she wore rubber heels.

"You will admit you were talking, I suppose, Marianna?" she inquired.

"Certainly I will admit it. I was talking. I don't crawl, Miss Hale." And Polly sucked in her under lip, a danger sign that she was angry.

"I was talking, too, Miss Hale," spoke up Lois.

The Spartan paid no attention to this, however, but marched off down the corridor. Two minutes later she confronted them in Latin class. Polly was still sucking in her under lip.

"Papers for the day on my desk, *if* you please."

"My Latin is unprepared," announced Polly with deadly calm. "And," she added, "I have no excuse."

"Dear me!" And Miss Hale raised her eyebrows until they disappeared into the depths of her large pompadour. "And is there any other girl whose Latin is not prepared, and who had no excuse?" she inquired.

As no one answered she continued:

"And may I ask why your Latin is not prepared? Don't you like Latin, Marianna?"

"No, I do not, Miss Hale," Polly answered, dangerously polite.

"You don't like Latin, so you don't prepare Latin; how very unfortunate!"

"I never said that was the reason I was unprepared. I told you I had no excuse."

Polly was getting very angry, still she might have controlled herself if just at that moment Miss Hale had not lifted a restraining hand and said, "Tut, my dear," in her most irritating manner.

Have you ever noticed the effect "Tut, tut," has on an angry person? Sometimes it's quite dreadful. Polly was no exception. She stamped her foot, threw her Latin book violently on the floor and marched out of the room, slamming the door behind her.

Punishment followed as a matter of course. Polly had expected to be sent to Mrs. Baird. She did not know how thoroughly the Spartan disapproved of her superior's gentle lectures, preferring more drastic measures.

It was not until after school, however, that she learned her fate. It was in the shape of a note that read as follows:

"Kindly keep silence for the afternoon; report in the study hall and make up today's lesson, the advance lesson, and translate the first ten lines of story on page 35. Bring work to my room."

"Hard luck," sympathized Lois, reading over Polly's shoulder. "That means no coasting. I wish I could help you." Then putting her arm around her. "There, dear, never mind, don't cry."

"I'm not," denied Polly, hastily daubing at her eyes, "but if you stay here any longer, I will. Go on, or I'll blub."

Lois left to hunt up Betty, who had completely recovered from her ducking and again grinned joyously on the world. Together they went out to coast. As they passed the bulletin board Lois stopped and read:

There will be a lecture on anatomy, by Miss F. Tilden-Brown, in Assembly Hall, at 8 P. M. tonight.

"The dickens there will," exclaimed Betty. "Anatomy forsooth, and by Miss Tilden-Brown. Nothing a woman with a name like that could say would interest me."

"That's right, think of yourself instead of poor Polly. Latin all afternoon and anatomy all evening."

Betty looked thoughtful.

"Hum; she's already in a sweet temper," she mused. "I see trouble ahead."

At 4:30 Polly, with her finished papers in her hand, crossed the Bridge of Sighs and knocked at Miss Hale's door.

"Come in," called that lady.

She was attired in a flowered kimono and was in the act of brushing her mouse-colored hair.

"My papers, Miss Hale," announced Polly in her most frigid tones.

"Very well, if you will put them on my table, please." Then as she turned to leave the room the demon in the Spartan prompted her to add: "Have you nothing to say? You know it is customary when one has thrown books about, to—"

"Oh, an apology," interrupted Polly. "I suppose Mrs. Baird would wish it." And looking straight into Miss Hale's watery blue eyes, she said: "I apologize."

It was insolence, of course, but, after all, an entire afternoon of Latin demands some outlet.

As Polly reached the corridor, Lois and Betty met her.

"Poor darling, are you awfully tired?" Lois asked. "We did miss you so; the coasting was—" but Polly interrupted her.

"Lois, if you dare tell me what a good time you had I'll never speak to you again." Then as she saw her surprised look, she added, laughing: "Don't get worried, I'm just awfully cranky and my head is splitting."

"Better wash your face in cold water," suggested Betty, "and stop thinking of Latin. For instance, contemplate the joys of this evening in the arms of Miss Tilden-Brown and anatomy."

"What!" yelled Polly. "A lecture tonight. Oh, that's too much. I'm going to cut," she announced.

There was silence for a full minute. They had reached Polly's room by now. Then Lois said very solemnly:

"I've never cut before, but if you're determined to do it, I'll go with you."

"So will I," echoed Betty, springing up from the window seat. "I'd brave anything—lions, Cæsar's ghost, or the whale that swallowed Jonah—rather than listen to that lecture. Besides, I couldn't desert you, Polly. Where will we go?"

"Coasting, of course," Polly answered. "There's a gorgeous moon."

"We will be caught," remarked Lois, "but then we're all willing to face the consequences."

That evening at 8:15 when the girls were all seated in Assembly Hall and Miss Tilden-Brown was expatiating on the evil results of tight lacing, three figures, standing on top of the hill, were silhouetted against the sky.

The moon was there, as Polly had predicted, making the snow sparkle with its blue-white rays. The silence was broken only by the crunch, crunch of the snow, as the three girls pulled their sleds into place.

"You go first, Polly," said Bet. "It's your party, and we'll follow close behind so the goblins won't get you."

"I'm off, then," and Polly threw herself flat on her sled.

It was great sport. The track was so icy that the runners made sparks as the sleds whizzed down the steep hill.

About nine o'clock Mrs. Baird stole from the Assembly Hall and sought the rest of her own room. She had grown fearfully tired of Miss Tilden-Brown's endless talk, and heartily sorry for the girls.

As she reached her dainty chintz-hung sitting-room, she lifted the window and stood looking at the big full moon and breathing the cool night air. Presently a joyous laugh rang out, followed by another. Mrs. Baird looked puzzled and leaned farther out of the window.

The laugh had been caused by Betty forgetting to steer and tumbling into a snow bank, thereby blocking the way for Polly and Lois, who were following close behind, so that they all landed in the drift.

"Somebody pull me out," sang Polly.

"Sorry, can't oblige," came Lois' muffled tones. "I'm on my way to China."

"Betty to the rescue. Whose foot is this?"

"Ouch! Oh, let go!"

"That was a mix-up."

"Where are the sleds?"

After much scrambling they managed to regain the track.

"Lucky thing we were not all killed," Betty reflected.

"Serve us right for cutting," commented Lois.

"'Bout time to go in, isn't it?" Polly inquired regretfully.

"Yes, it's all over," replied Betty. "And now the consequences. Wonder what part of the anatomy Miss Tilden-Brown is discussing now?" And she chuckled gleefully.

Mrs. Baird smiled broadly and closed the window. A few minutes later she met the girls in the lower hall.

"Why, girls, where have you been?" she inquired.

"Out coasting, Mrs. Baird," Lois answered. "We cut the lecture," she added, nervously twisting the third finger of her red mitten.

"Perhaps you had better come into my office and tell me about it," suggested Mrs. Baird, and she led the way down the hall.

They were in the office just ten minutes, but in that time Mrs. Baird found out all she wanted to know. Polly's afternoon in the study hall, Betty's dislike for lectures, and Lois' love for adventure. She finished the interview with these words:

"I did not expect it of you girls in the past, and I am not going to expect it of you in the future. I look to you as holding the position of wholesome examples in the school. Your fault tonight was not very great, but it was a step in the wrong direction. Pull yourselves up, and now, good-night."

As the girls turned to go, she added with a smile:

"I promise you all, there will be no more lectures on anatomy."

They walked thoughtfully back to the corridor. As Betty opened her door she said:

"For two years I've been trying to find an adjective to describe Mrs. Baird and the nearest I can come to one is 'saint,' and that doesn't suit her at all. Good-night."

"Good-night," answered Polly. "I suppose there will be no more cutting."

"No, I suppose not," agreed Lois, "but, cricky, I wouldn't have missed tonight."

They all laughed guiltily, and then as they heard the rest of the girls trooping out of Assembly Hall, stole quietly into their rooms.

An hour later Miss Hale and Mrs. Baird were alone in the faculty room, finishing a conversation.

"I can't understand," Mrs. Baird was saying, "why, when you bend a girl to the breaking point, you are surprised that she breaks. You know it is near Christmas and they are all tired."

"Our ideas of discipline are very different," Miss Hale returned stiffly.

"Well, after all, you will admit I am the head of the school," Mrs. Baird reminded her, smiling good-naturedly to soften the rebuke.

"Certainly, to be sure," Miss Hale stammered, rather lamely. "I think I'll be saying good-night."

When she had gone, Mrs. Baird sank into a big chair before the hearth.

"It was breaking rules, of course," she mused, smiling into the fire, "but I can't help loving them for wanting to coast instead of listening to anatomy lectures. It shows they've healthy minds anyway, bless them."

CHAPTER IX—THE CHRISTMAS HOLIDAYS

The first day of the Xmas holidays had at last arrived and fifty-six tired girls were busily packing trunks and bags. Nerves that had been overstrained for the past couple of weeks had relaxed, and everywhere there was the noise and excitement of leaving.

In Freshman corridor trunks were being jumped on and made to close, and all the girls were exchanging addresses and exacting promises of letters and visits.

"Oh, Lois," sighed Polly, taking her chum's arm and leading her to the end of the corridor farthest away from the rest of the girls, "I do wish you didn't live in Albany. Of course I'll be glad to see Uncle Roddy, but I can't help feeling that vacation is going to be awful lonely."

"I know," replied Lois. "I wish we could be together; anyhow we can write. Bet will be in New York and you will see her."

"Yes, but Bet's not you," Polly answered. "But let's cheer up. Why, here's Betty now; speak of angels—looking for us?" she called.

"Oh, there you are; you're both wanted—Polly in the reception-room and Lo in Mrs. Baird's office."

"Do you know what for?"

"No." But Betty's expression made both girls apprehensive.

"Wonder what's up," queried Lois as they ran down the broad staircase to the main hall.

When Polly reached the reception hall she found Uncle Roddy with a big fur coat over his arm, a cap in his hand, waiting for her.

"Hello, Tiddle-dy-winks; thought I'd plan a surprise for you, so I came up in the motor to take you home. It's a glorious day. If there are any girls you care to bring along, why—"

But Uncle Roddy's explanation of his unexpected arrival was cut short by Polly's violent hug and kiss.

"Uncle Roddy, what a darling you are!" she exclaimed. "I'll get ready this minute and see who I can get to go with us." And she flew back to the corridor.

As she stood in her room throwing the remaining leftovers into her trunk, Lois came in and threw herself on the bed, in tears.

"Polly, Bobbie has typhoid and I can't go home," she sobbed. "Father wired Mrs. Baird. Poor darling Bob!" Her voice was muffled in the pillow.

Polly's joy in Uncle Roddy's surprise was forgotten as she tried to comfort her friend.

After Lois had left the office, Mrs. Baird returned to the reception-room where she had left Uncle Roddy.

"Did Marianna find you all right, Mr. Pendleton?" she asked. "Such a distressing thing has just happened! Dr. Farwell wired me that his son has

42

typhoid and Lois will have to remain here for the vacation. I am sorry, for the child needed a change."

Then it was that Uncle Roddy had an inspiration. The thought of amusing Polly during the vacation had worried him. Several ladies of his acquaintance had promised to take her about, but that had not reassured him. Now if there were two of them, they would amuse each other, and under the able care of Mrs. Bent, his worthy housekeeper, all would be well.

It was a matter of a few minutes to lay the plan before Mrs. Baird and, with her help, to reach Dr. Farwell by long distance telephone. Over the wire the two men renewed their acquaintance of college days and the doctor was only too delighted to give his consent.

In less than an hour the two girls were wrapped up in countless fur robes in the back seat of Uncle Roddy's comfortable car, while that relieved gentleman was at the wheel, and the chauffeur, always along in case of tire trouble, occupied the seat beside him.

As it was twelve o'clock when they started, Uncle Roddy suggested luncheon at the hotel in the village. That was lark number one. The food was terrible, but Uncle Roddy was so funny the way he imitated the waiter and teased the big green parrot, that as long as the food was filling, it didn't matter about the taste.

On the road they had two tires blow out, and as the second happened just on the outskirts of Irvington-on-the-Hudson, home of Rip Van Winkle, Uncle Roddy suggested dinner at the Sleepy Hollow Inn. They had the most delicious muffins, and pork chops with apple sauce, and very black coffee. That was lark number two.

But best of all was the getting home at ten o'clock. Uncle Roddy lived on Riverside Drive in a big apartment, with Mr. and Mrs. Bent, his housekeeper and butler.

Polly had stayed with him for three months before going to school and knew the lay of the land. She led the way to the big guest room that she had occupied, but instead of the gray walls and sedate old mahogany furniture that she remembered, imagine her surprise at finding soft cream walls with a border of nodding yellow daffodils and the most adorable ivory-colored furniture.

Lois broke the amazed silence by demanding:

"Polly, what a beautiful room; why did you never tell me about it?"

But Polly was speechless with delight as she stood looking, first at the big double bed with the carved roses at the head and foot and next at the dressing-table with its dainty silver brushes and combs and Dresden china candlesticks. A slender-legged table with a bowl of yellow tea-roses on it stood beside the bed, and the walls were hung with colored prints of Greuze's "Girl with the Broken Pitcher" and "The Milk Maid," Reynolds' darling portrait of "Penelope" and "The Boy with the Rabbit."

Polly, in the days of Aunt Hannah and her four-posted beds and crazy quilts, had dreamed of a room such as this. Finally she managed to answer Lois' question.

"I didn't know about it myself, till this very minute," she gasped. "Oh, Uncle Roddy, it's beautiful! I never saw anything half so lovely!"

"I wanted you to feel at home, dear child, and now I think you had both better get to sleep." And after renewed thanks and good-night kisses, he left them.

A second later Mrs. Bent tiptoed in with a broad smile that took in the whole world.

"You're hungry, I'm sure, my dears. I'll have some hot chocolate ready for you when you get into bed; just ring when you want it."

Polly and Lois hugged each other for joy and after taking a disgracefully long time to undress, they finally fell asleep over their chocolate and cakes.

The two weeks of Christmas vacation was an unending good time; every minute was full. The mornings were spent chiefly in bed, for Mrs. Bent brought them their breakfast and sat to chat.

Sometimes they lunched down-town with Uncle Roddy and sometimes they motored through Central Park, or, with Mrs. Bent for chaperone, wandered through the stores, and as the old Scotch woman could refuse them nothing, they did pretty much as they chose.

Uncle Roddy came home at four o'clock and always with bonbons and theater tickets.

It would be useless to try and recount all their doings, so you will have to be contented with the descriptions of the good times that pleased them most.

One was Lois' box party for "Peter Pan." Dr. Farwell had written that the seats were in her name at the box office for Saturday matinée, and the question arose whom to ask.

"There's Betty, of course," said Lois. "We'll phone her this morning; and Angela and Connie live in New Jersey and we ought to be able to get them."

Betty's home was reached and her voice sounded over the wire in reply to Lois' invitation:

"Come? You bet I will! What a lark!"

"Ask her for luncheon," called Polly. Then hurriedly to Mrs. Bent: "It will be all right, won't it?"

"Indeed it will, my lamb; any one you like; it's only too happy I am to see a little life now and then," answered that devoted woman.

When the receiver was hung up it was arranged that Betty would be at the apartment Saturday morning. Angela and Connie had another engagement and couldn't possibly come.

"That's too bad, Lo. Who can you ask now?"

Lois looked puzzled for a minute and then exclaimed:

"I have it! Why can't Uncle Roddy" (she had called him Uncle since the dinner at the Sleepy Hollow Inn), "and that funny man, Mr. Whittington, ⸱e?"

No sooner said than done. The long-suffering operator connected them with the office in Wall Street occupied by George B. Whittington, broker. He was a little taken back at the invitation, but answered that he would be "pleased as punch and would meet them at the theater." Uncle Roddy also accepted with pleasure.

Betty arrived Saturday morning, and the three of them chattered like magpies until luncheon. They drove to the theater in the motor and found the two men there to meet them. Betty was introduced to Mr. Whittington and she nicknamed him The Lord Mayor of London at once, after Dick of the same name in the nursery tales. By the time the curtain went up they were the best of friends.

Of course they adored *Peter Pan* and *Wendy*. They laughed a good deal and cried a little and waved their handkerchiefs madly when *Peter* asked them if they believed in fairies.

"This is quite the nicest party I ever attended," Mr. Whittington insisted as the curtain fell after the last act. "Why can't we have another one just like it, soon?"

"But, Mr. Lord Mayor of London," interrupted Betty, "where would we ever find another *Peter Pan?*"

"Just leave that to me. I know the very thing, but I'm not going to tell you a word about it. You must all be my guests for next Wednesday night. How about it?"

Everybody was of course delighted and accepted at once.

Wednesday night finally arrived and with it another jolly party. Mr. Whittington's surprise turned out to be the Russian Ballet, and as the girls watched the fascinating première danseuse as *Pupin Fee* (fairy doll) in that charming story dance, they were wild with delight, and Polly openly transferred her affection from *Peter Pan*. Lois remained faithful, and Betty never could make up her mind which one she loved the better.

"She might just as well be talking," exclaimed Polly between acts. "I know just what she's thinking with every move she makes. Oh, isn't she precious!"

"I know what the next composition I write for Miss Porter will be about," announced Betty.

"Oh, Bet, for pity sake stop talking about school. I'm in fairy land and I don't want to come back," Lois begged. "There goes the curtain up for the last act."

The evening was over far too soon to please our party and when Mr. Whittington said good-night, at the door of the theater, his guests left no doubt in his mind of their appreciation and enjoyment of the good time he had given them.

Best of all days of the vacation was Christmas. Polly and Lois were wakened at nine o'clock by Uncle Roddy's knock.

"Get up, you lazy children! Merry Christmas!" he called. "Lois, I have your mother on the phone for you. Come and speak to her."

Lois jumped out of bed and in a minute was calling Xmas greetings all the way to Albany.

45

After breakfast Mr. Whittington arrived, and he and Uncle Roddy whispered mysteriously. Finally Mr. Whittington said:

"Get your things on, girls; we're going for a ride."

"A ride?" exclaimed Polly. "Why, the ground's covered with snow."

"Doesn't make any difference; we're going for a ride," he told her and not another word could they get out of him.

They rode in the car as far as Fort Lee Ferry and then Uncle Roddy ordered them out, and they crossed the ice-choked Hudson on the ferry-boat.

"Please tell us where we are going," pleaded Polly.

"I am simply dying to know; it's all so mysterious," added Lois.

But "wait and see" was all the satisfaction they could get from Mr. Whittington and Uncle Roddy, and they had to wait until they reached Fort Lee, where a big double-seated sleigh was waiting for them.

When they were all in and the warm robes were tucked snugly about them, Mr. Whittington whipped up the two black horses and they were off along the smooth snow-covered road.

It was one o'clock before they finally reached an old-fashioned farmhouse way up in the hills back of the Hudson.

"Every one out!" ordered Uncle Roddy.

"What a ducky old house! But what are we here for?" asked Lois.

"I know," laughed Polly, stamping her feet on the porch. "An old-fashioned Xmas dinner."

"Quite right, Polly, and I hope it's a good one, for I'm starved. But here are Mr. and Mrs. Hopper, let's ask them about it."

As Mr. Whittington was speaking the door had opened and an old lady and gentleman stood in the hall.

"Merry Xmas to you both," he continued, shaking them each by the hand. "Let me introduce you to the rest. Girls, this is Mrs. John Samuel Hopper, the finest cook in the State of New York; every chance I get to eat one of her turkeys— well, I take it," he explained.

The old lady blushed with pleasure.

"Won't you be coming in?" she invited. "The dinner's ready, so you'd best set."

You may be sure they all did justice to the roast duck and turkey, for their ride had given them hearty appetites.

After dinner they went out to inspect the farm and ended by having a royal snow fight. When it was over Uncle Roddy suggested more to eat and they spent the rest of the afternoon before the open fire, roasting chestnuts and apples, while the men entertained them with stories of their college days.

The vacation ended at last and Uncle Roddy saw them off, each with a box of candy and a bunch of violets, at the Grand Central Station.

ʻldon Hall had a private car for the girls and as each one entered they were
ʻʸᵛ a chorus of shouts:

"Hello, did you have a good time?"

"So sorry I couldn't come and see you that day."

"Why didn't you answer my letter?"

"Didn't you adore 'Peter Pan'?" and a thousand other questions.

They reached school at six o'clock and as Polly and Lois strolled down the corridor, waiting for the supper bell, Lois said:

"Well, here we are, back again. Polly, I never had such a good time. I'll never be able to thank you."

"Oh, bother the thanks," replied Polly. "Do you know, Lois, now that we're back I feel as if we had never been away."

"I know," Lois sighed regretfully. "It's more like a wonderful dream. Still it is good to be back, you know it is."

"Of course it is," Polly agreed heartily.

Just then the gong rang and they went down to supper.

CHAPTER X—THE VALENTINE PARTY

On the twelfth of February, Mrs. Baird announced after school, that there would be a masquerade party on Valentine's Day.

"Last year, the old girls will remember, that we had a book party, and it was great fun," she said, "but this year, I have thought of something entirely new. I want you all to dress as famous women in history. Choose the particular heroine you admire most, find a picture of her in the library, and try to copy it. The attic will be open this afternoon and you may take what you want from the costume trunks. The Seniors have the affair in charge and they are offering a prize for the best representation." The girls clapped their appreciation of this novel idea and Mrs. Baird continued:

"Don't all come as Queen Elizabeths, and Betsy Rosses, find some one not so well known, and whom you really admire. There will be lots of visitors on the platform and I want you all to look your best."

"Jemima," Betty gasped, when they had been dismissed and she, Lois and Polly were in the latter's room. "Who under the sun can we go as?"

"It is hard, isn't it?" Lois said, "but you had a splendid costume last year; didn't you go as the Last of the Mohicans?"

"Yes, I have my Indian suit."

"Why don't you go as Pocahontas?" Polly suggested. "Your hair isn't black, but it would look great in two heavy braids."

"That's just what I'll do. I'll go grab that suit before any of the others get it." And Betty dashed for the attic.

Lois jumped as the door slammed. "Isn't that just like Bet, she ought to go as a little whirlwind. Poll, what can we go as?"

"I don't know, let's ask Miss Porter."

"Do you suppose we can find her?"

"Yes, she's probably in her room."

They walked down Faculty Corridor, and tapped gently at the last door on the left.

"Come in," called a voice, not Miss Porter's.

They entered, to find Miss King, the trained nurse, sitting on the window box, a bunch of artificial flowers in one hand, and a rather battered velvet hat in the other.

"Is Miss Porter here?" Lois asked.

"Yes, just a minute," Miss Porter was struggling in the depths of her closet. "I'll be with you in a second; sit down."

"What is it, costumes?" Miss King asked, when they were seated on the couch.

"Yes, we thought Miss Porter would help us decide what to wear," Polly explained.

"I'm here about costumes, too, but it's hardly the same. I'm begging. I found that poor little wretch Martha, who works in the laundry, out yesterday without a hat. I told her she'd catch her death of cold and to go put one on right away. She said she couldn't because she didn't have any."

"Oh, the poor kid," Polly's sympathy was genuine.

"I've a tam I could give her to wear every day," she said shyly, "if you think—"

"Think, I know she'd love it. I'll come to your room and get it after you've had your talk with Miss Porter. Thank you. I was trying to rig up something out of these," she shook the flowers and hat, "but a tam will save the day."

While this conversation was going on, Lois had been explaining their difficulty to Miss Porter.

"'Women in History.' That ought to be easy." Miss Porter thought for a minute. "Mrs. Baird really wants you to go as your favorite characters? Lois, who is your favorite heroine?"

"Jeanne d'Arc, the martyred Maid of Orleans," Lois replied dramatically. "Do you think I might go as Jeanne d'Arc?" she asked eagerly.

"I like that," Polly interrupted. "I thought at the Hallow-e'en party I was to be a Jeanne d'Arc. Oh, well, I give up my rights for this once; besides," she added seriously, "I don't really love her the way you do."

"Won't armor be hard to imitate?" Miss King asked.

Miss Porter walked over beside the window and took down a framed picture from the wall. She held it behind her back.

"Armor won't be necessary," she said. "Lois, have you ever seen the Jeanne d'Arc painting by Jules Bastien-Lepage, at the Metropolitan Museum in New York City?"

"Oh, yes, of course, I saw it this vacation. She's standing in the woods, just in peasant clothes. I love it. She looks as if she were seeing visions. You remember it, Poll?" Lois was all excitement.

"Here's a copy of it," Miss Porter said, producing the picture. "And Lois, I declare you look like her. There, you may keep this print to refer to, it ought to be very easy to find a peasant's costume. Now Polly, who's your favorite heroine?"

Polly rumpled her hair, hesitated, and rumpled her hair again.

"She's not very well known, at least, I never heard any one talk about her," she answered, "but I think she's the bravest woman that ever lived. We had a book about her at home, that I used to read and re-read on rainy days."

"Well, what's her name?" Lois demanded impatiently.

"Florence Nightingale, the Angel of the Crimea," Polly said, very solemnly.

"Oh, Polly, do you love her, too?" Miss King's eyes were shining. "So do I."

"You couldn't choose a better woman to portray, dear child," Miss Porter spoke up. "You'll find the Seniors know all about her. They are studying about the Crimean War this winter."

"Please tell me who she was, I never even heard of her," said Lois apologetically.

Miss King began: "She was an Englishwoman, the first one to go out as a nurse for the soldiers. She thought that if they fought for their country, the least their country could do for them was to give them proper care when they were wounded. At first the generals resented her interfering and thought she was fussy because she wanted clean hospitals and clean food—"

"But the soldiers adored her," Polly interrupted, and then carried away by the theme, she continued. "She always walked through the long hospital wards every night and they used to turn and kiss her shadow on the wall as she passed, and they named her the Angel of the Crimea. Oh, she was so brave. All the hardships she went through, cold and hunger." Polly stopped speaking, but her thoughts went back to the stirring scenes she had read about and thrilled over so often in a certain little window seat off the broad stairway in her old home.

Miss King's voice recalled her, "I can give you a costume, one of my 'kerchiefs will do, and I know how to make a Nightingale cap. We'll part your hair in the middle and fix it low on your neck and—"

They took the rest of the afternoon to discuss the plans. It was not until the dressing hour that Polly and Lois saw Betty again. She had apparently found her costume without any trouble, for she had been skating all afternoon.

"The ice was bully," she greeted them. "Where have you been all this time?"

"With Miss Porter; did you find your costume?" Polly answered.

"Yes, first thing. Have you decided what you're going as?"

"Yes, but we're not telling," Lois teased. "We thought out peachy ones."

"Ah, please."

"No, never."

"Do you know what any of the others are going as?"

The conversation was being shouted from room to room.

"No, do you?"

"Connie is going as Lady Macbeth."

"What, why she's not historical, she's Shakespearean," Polly protested.

49

"Connie insists she was a real woman, and that Shakespeare knew all about her. Anyway, she says she's going to walk in her sleep and say: 'Out, damned spot.'"

"Are you really, Con?" Lois raised her voice so that it could be heard at the other end of the corridor.

"Am I really what?" came Connie's reply.

"Going as Lady Macbeth at the party?"

"Of course I am. She was a real person."

"Well, she wasn't very well known," Angela added her voice to the others.

"Maybe not, to the uneducated," Connie said loftily, "but she will be after the party."

There was a minute of hilarious laughter, that ended as the study hour bell rang for silence.

After dinner, Lois and Polly, their weighty problem of costumes off their minds, were talking of valentines.

"If we could only think of something different, there are no really good ones at the store," Lois said, rummaging in the closet for the peanut butter jar.

"I know it. I bought some but they are no good. How do you send them, through the mails?" Polly asked.

"No, the Seniors make a big red box and put it in the Assembly Room valentine morning, and everybody puts their letters in it. The box is opened at the party and the valentines are given out."

"How would it be to make some red cardboard hearts and write verses on them?"

"Make them up, do you mean?"

"Yes, about the girls."

"Fine, let's try—but first let's get comfy."

Lois' definition of comfy was to sit tailor fashion on a bed surrounded by pillows, with jam, crackers and other eatables near at hand.

Polly preferred the window seat, it was broad and cozy, and you could always look out of the window when you wanted inspiration.

"All ready," Lois said, sitting down. "Give me a pencil. Now, who first?"

"You take Bet, and I'll take Connie," Polly said.

They both wrote for a minute, and then Lois read:

"Oh, Betty Thompson, Betty B.,
When you get this please think of me
No, that's no good."

"It is good," Polly protested feebly, "but it's not especially original."

"That's awful," Lois insisted, drawing a heavy line through the words.

"What's yours to Connie?"

"To Connie, our musician, a valentine we send,

50

We hope that when she gets this she will her manners mend."

"That rimes," Lois said reluctantly. "But there's nothing the matter with Con's manners, so it doesn't make sense."

"That's just it," Polly agreed hopelessly. "We can't write sense that rimes, because we're not poets."

"Betty can, let's get her to help. You go, I'm so comfy."

"All right, lazy one, don't eat all the jam before I get back," and Polly left, to return in a few minutes with Betty.

"Original valentines, that's a bully idea," she said when the plan had been explained to her. "Let's start with Connie."

Polly and Lois agreed. They did not think it necessary to say that they had already started with Connie.

"Four lines are enough, let's see, what rimes with valentine? Columbine, turpentine—aha! I've got it." Betty scribbled furiously. "How's this?

"Just to tell you, Connie,
That a drop of turpentine,
Will take the blood stain off your hand,
We send this valentine."

"Oh, Bet, that's great. How did you ever think of it?" Polly was filled with admiration.

"Oh, genius is burning tonight, that's all," Betty laughed. "Now let's think of one for Angela."

"Something about Latin for her, don't you think?" Polly said.

The suggestion was enough for Betty. "Fine, dine, pine," she chanted. "Listen:

"Angela, so fair and wise,
Oh hear us sadly pine,
We've tried, but couldn't find you
A Latin valentine."

Lois and Polly looked at each other in speechless wonder, and Betty, now thoroughly started, wrote absurd jingles to all the girls. She reached the height of her achievement in Louise Preston.

"Read it again, Bet, it's the best of all," Polly said, delighted. And Lois spread a cracker inches thick with jam, and presented it—

"To the Poet," she said. "I haven't a laurel wreath so this will have to do."

"You can't eat it until you've read the poem again," Polly insisted.

"Oh, all right." Betty consulted her pad.

"Some people sigh, and wish for the day,
When work is all gone, and there's only play.
But if the world were black as ink,
We wouldn't care at all
If Lois were always captain

And our hearts her basket ball."

"I don't think much of it, the meter changes," Betty said critically.

"That's all right, as long as it doesn't change in the same verse," Polly replied. "I think it's great. Who next?"

"Oh, no more tonight," Betty groaned, "give me my cracker. I'm starved."

"No time, there goes the silence bell." Lois laughed.

"No time? Just watch me," and Betty put the whole cracker in her mouth at once, and left for her own room.

"Good-night," Polly and Lois called after her, but she could only nod in response.

The party was at its height. Every age and every country was represented in the costumes. Betsy Rosses, Grace Darlings and Pocahontases abounded among the younger children. And there was every known character from Agrippa of Roman fame, to Queen Victoria, among the upper school. High ruffs danced with 'kerchiefs, and French heels, with sandals. In fact, every one had taken so much interest in their costume that the Seniors and faculty, who were acting as judges, were hard put to find any one particular girl who outshone the rest.

Lois and Betty had drifted off to a corner of the room, during the refreshments. They made a curious picture against the boughs of green that decked the walls. Betty was a stolid Indian maid, from the beaded moccasins to her parted hair, her face was smeared with grease paint, and she had tribal marks all over her forehead and cheeks. Polly looked very efficient in her immaculate nurse's costume, her hair was parted severely, and she had on a soft white winged cap. Over her uniform she wore a long gray cape. No one had been able to name her, and after the guessing was over she spent her time in explaining, and exalting Florence Nightingale.

As for Lois, Miss Porter was right when she said that she looked like Bastien-Lepage's picture of Jeanne d'Arc, and certainly rags became her. She had found a bodice, that laced over a white blouse, and an old patched skirt. Miss Porter had fixed her hair in a soft careless knot, and as she stood beside Polly and Betty, a little tired from the excitement of the evening, there was a far away, dreamy look in her eyes that bespoke the seeing of glorious visions.

"Louise asked me if we sent her that valentine," Lois said, between sips of lemonade.

"Did you tell her we did?" Polly inquired.

"Yes, I did, because she said it was the sweetest one she'd received, and I just had to let her know that Bet wrote it."

Betty said: "Oh, shucks, why did you do that?" and changed the subject by asking: "Who do you think will get the prize?"

The answer was cut short as Angela, who was Catharine of Russia, and Connie joined them.

"Well, Lady Macbeth," Polly greeted them, "have you established your claim to being a real historical character yet?"

52

"I have, doubter," Connie answered haughtily. "There was a real Lady Macbeth, Mrs. Baird says so, and, 'sure she is an honorable man, woman,' I mean, 'Therefore, avaunt and quit my sight, let the earth hide thee, and thy base mockery.'"

Angela put her hand over Connie's mouth. "Don't mind her, she's been talking like this all evening," she said. "Did you get the packages that were in the express-room?"

"Packages, no, where are they?" Polly demanded.

"Why, I saw them before dinner, there were three, just alike, and addressed to you and Lo, and Bet."

"Let's get them this minute," Betty said, starting for the door. "Come on with us."

They threaded their way through the crowd of dancing girls, and raced for the express-room.

"I bet it's a joke," Lois said as she reached for the electric switch.

But when the light was turned on, sure enough there were three packages, piled one on the other, on the table.

"Open them quick," Connie commanded. "I am dying of curiosity."

Off came the wrappers, and there was a shout of joy as three heart-shaped boxes of candy appeared.

"How wonderful!"

"My favorite kind!"

"What adorable boxes!"

"They're painted on silk."

"How sweet!"

"Who could have sent them?" Lois asked.

"Mr. Pendleton, perhaps," Betty suggested.

"No, it's not Uncle Roddy's writing," Polly said; "besides, he sent me a little gold heart, yesterday."

"Open them, perhaps there's a card or something inside," Angela suggested. This proved to be the case.

Polly opened hers first, and the rest watched eagerly.

"It just says: 'A friend of a very dear friend of yours,'" she read. "Who can that be? Read yours, Lo."

"Mine says: 'In remembrance of a charming evening.'"

"Listen, I know," Betty exclaimed. "'From a devoted admirer, once mayor of a certain city.' Don't you see, it's Mr. Whittington, that friend of your uncle's, Polly."

"Of course it is, and the very dear friend of mine is Uncle Roddy," Polly exclaimed delightedly.

"The charming evening must be the night we went to see 'Peter Pan,'" Lois said. "Wasn't it nice of him to remember it."

"But why does he say 'once mayor of a certain city'?" Connie inquired, re-reading Betty's card.

"Oh, that's because Bet nicknamed him Lord Mayor of London," Polly explained. "His name is really Dick Whittington."

They each selected a candy, and munched in happy silence.

"Lois Farwell, Lois Farwell. Oh, Lois," a voice called suddenly from the depths of the hall. "Where are you?"

"Here, in the express-room," Lois answered; "What is it?"

Dot Mead poked her head in the doorway.

"You're wanted upstairs, right away, hurry!"

"Why?" chorused everybody.

"Oh, never mind," Dot said, mysteriously, "only hurry."

They were no sooner in the Assembly Hall again before Mrs. Baird tapped the little desk bell for silence.

"Girls, the Seniors have decided to award the prize of the evening to Jeanne D'Arc, impersonated by Lois Farwell. Lois, will you come here, dear?"

The girls made an opening through the center of the room. Lois, too mystified for words, walked slowly up to the platform. Mrs. Baird presented her with a tiny silver loving cup. "This gives me very great pleasure, my dear," she said smiling, "because Jeanne D'Arc is one of my favorite heroines, too."

Lois tried to stammer her thanks. Just then Louise Preston stepped forward with a wreath of laurel. "Here's the crown that goes with it, Lo," she whispered. "Kneel down."

Lois knelt on the lower step, and Louise placed the wreath on her head.

"I crown you the most beautiful picture of the evening," she said. And the girls broke out in heartiest applause.

"I knew it, I knew it," Miss Porter whispered to Miss King. "She's exquisite. See how her eyes sparkle when she blushes. She's exactly the sensitive, delicate type, for a Jeanne D'Arc."

"She is lovely," Miss King agreed, in her frank way. "But if I'd had the awarding of the prize, Polly would have had it. She's a splendid girl, she gave me a sweater, as well as a tam for Martha. I love that spirit."

Lois went to bed, elated at her success, and the praise she had received. She smiled delightedly at her reflection in the mirror.

"I wonder," she mused, "if any one will ever tell Mother about this. I would like her to know but, of course, I can't myself."

CHAPTER XI—PRACTICING FOR THE INDOOR MEET

The last bell had just sounded and the girls were leaving the schoolroom for the day. Two weeks had passed since the Valentine party. Today was Wednesday and the coming Saturday was the date fixed for the Indoor Meet.

The Whitehead School basket-ball team was to meet the Seddon Hall girls for their annual game. The year before they had played at Whitehead and were beaten. This year the game was to be played at Seddon Hall and the girls were determined there should be no more defeats.

"Wait a minute, you two," called Connie, as she and Angela caught up with Polly and Lois in the schoolroom corridor. "I've news; such news!"

"What is it?" inquired Lois, in the act of retying Polly's hair ribbon.

"Don't breathe a word about it. I don't suppose Louise Preston wants it known all over the school," answered Connie. "But as I was going through Senior Corridor to my music lesson, I heard her say to Gladys Couch (jumping center on the big team): 'Then you won't be here for Saturday?' And Glid said: 'Isn't it awful, Louise, but I don't see how I can possibly get back before Monday.' Well, of course, Polly, you know what that means."

"What's the giddy secret?" sang out Betty, coming towards them from one of the classrooms.

"Bet, oh, Bet, catch me quick!" cried Polly, falling into her arms in a mock faint. "Such news! Tell her, some one, quick!"

"Wah!" exclaimed Betty when she had heard. "You'll have to play on the big team, Polly. Isn't that bully!"

As they all stood talking it over, in subdued whispers, Louise Preston appeared at the other end of the corridor.

"Oh, Polly," she called, "can you spare me a few minutes? Let's go in this classroom; then we won't be disturbed."

She put her arm around Polly's shoulder as she had done the first day. Once inside the classroom, she began:

"We've had some pretty bad news this morning. Gladys Couch received a telegram that her brother is going to be married on Saturday. Well, of course, Glid will have to go home. She can't very well ask them to postpone the wedding," she added, smiling, "and that leaves us without a jumping center. Polly, you know we simply must win this game. You'll have to play and you'll have to play as you never played before. Better get some practicing in and, remember, I'm depending on you."

She was gone before Polly could realize what had happened. She spent the rest of the day in the gym with Lois and Betty as Louise had suggested.

Misfortunes never come singly. The next day Flora Illington, the other substitute center, had a phone message that her father was very ill and she had to leave at once. Flora was just one of the girls at Seddon Hall; apart from her position on the team, she had no particular place in the school.

However, it was with genuine sympathy and feeling that the girls saw her leave and the week after heard of her father's death.

Flora never returned to school and after the letters of condolence were written and answered, she was forgotten.

Polly met Louise in the gym that afternoon.

"Isn't it dreadful about Flora?" she began.

"Yes, I hope there's nothing serious the matter with her father," Louise answered. Then with a sigh: "I suppose I'm a brute, but I can't help thinking, there goes another substitute."

"Cheer up," advised Polly, "she probably wouldn't have been needed. How are the songs getting along?"

"Wonderfully! Betty and Angela handed in two dandies today, but of course I'm looking to the Juniors for most of them."

"Well, so long."

"Don't work too hard, and don't you dare hurt yourself."

"I won't, and you cheer up."

Louise left the gym and Polly jumped into the game, calmly taking the ball out of Connie's astonished hands.

She worked furiously all afternoon and when next she had a minute to breathe she was back in her own room getting ready for her bath.

"I tell you, Polly," sang out Betty from across the hall, "you certainly played this afternoon."

"Hum!" Polly grumbled, screwing her hair up into a tight knot. "I made a nasty foul. Thank goodness Louise wasn't there."

"Aren't you two slow pokes ready for your baths yet?" demanded Lois, thumping on the door.

"Well, I can't find my slippers," Polly complained, rummaging under the bed. "Angela," she called, "darling Angela, please lend me your slippers."

"All right, here they come." And a pair of Chinese slippers flew through the transom.

"Thanks! Oh, I say, I asked for slippers, not stilts," Polly grumbled. "How do you keep the crazy things on?"

"Ingratitude, thy name is Polly," began Angela, but Polly was half way down the hall and out of hearing, with Lois and Betty. Lois was saying:

"How did you ever manage to make that foul?" And Polly explained, just as they came to the head of the stairs.

"Why, Connie had the ball and I jumped for it. She tried to pass it to Dot and I thought I could get it by batting it back, like this—"

She leaned forward to show what she meant, completely forgetting the stairs. Angela's slippers gave a half twist and she plunged headlong down the steps.

Miss King said her ankle was badly sprained and the doctor was summoned.

She lay on the infirmary bed, biting her lips and trying to keep back the tears. The doctor had strapped her ankle and told Miss King that she was not to put her foot to the ground for two weeks.

At last Louise's voice sounded outside the door.

"All right," she was saying. "I promise to stay only a second." And in a minute she was at Polly's side. It was more than the poor child could stand. She burst into tears and hid her face in the pillows.

"Oh, Louise," she sobbed, "can you ever forgive me? And you told me to be careful!"

"Why, honey child, you couldn't help it," comforted Louise. "Here, cheer up, you'll make yourself sick. Angela's downstairs tearing her hair out and swearing vengeance on her poor slippers."

"But the game! Who'll play in my place?" wailed Polly.

"That is just what I came up to talk to you about," Louise told her. "Can you suggest any one? We're stumped."

"Wouldn't Betty do? I know she'd be careful about fouls. Please give her a chance."

"I think perhaps you're right. I'll go and talk to her," Louise replied. "Be good, dear, and don't worry. I know it's a terrible disappointment." And she leaned over and kissed Polly's hot cheek.

"All right, I'll try. If you see Lois will you ask her to come up and talk to me? I'll go crazy if I have to stay here alone."

But it was not until some hours later that Lois appeared. Miss King thought solitude the best thing for Polly's feverish condition.

"You are a nice one," grumbled Polly when Lois entered the room. "I thought you were never coming near me again."

"Come near you! Why, I've been sitting outside Miss King's door all afternoon, waiting for permission to see you. Poor darling! How's the ankle? Awfully painful?" explained Lois.

"Do you mean to tell me Miss King wouldn't let you in before now?" demanded Polly.

"Yes; she said you were very feverish and she wanted you to rest; and for goodness' sake don't excite yourself or I'll have to leave; you must be kept quiet."

"And here I've been thinking you a cold-hearted wretch all afternoon. Just wait till I see Miss King!"

"What are you going to do to her?" asked that lady herself, poking her white-capped head around the corner of the door.

"Oh, there you are, eh?" laughed Polly. "Why wouldn't you let Lois come in before?"

"Because I'm a cross old thing," laughed Miss King. "But just to show you that I can be nice sometimes, if you have no more fever I'll let her stay and have supper with you. Now what am I?"

"You're a darling and I'll love you forever, but don't you dare find I have a fever," replied Polly.

Miss King did find her temperature a little above normal, but so little that Lois was permitted to stay, and the two of them had such a jolly time that Polly almost succeeded in forgetting the coming game and her own disappointment, and you may be sure Lois carefully kept off that dangerous subject. The time passed so quickly that the bell for study hour rang long before they expected it, and Lois had to fly to escape being late.

"Lo, half a minute," Betty called just before the good-night bell. "I've something to tell you. I am chosen to fill Polly's place tomorrow. Louise just told me."

"I'm awfully glad for you, Bet," answered Lois. "I know you'll make good, but—"

"Yes, it's that but that makes me so miserable," replied Betty. "How can I be excited and pleased when I know Polly's up there in the infirmary—Oh, it makes me sick to think of it!" she finished, and before Lois could reply, she had disappeared into her own room and closed the door.

"Poor Betty," sighed Lois sympathetically. "It's all a mean shame."

Just before Miss King turned out the infirmary lights, she delivered a note to Polly. It read:

"Polly Dear:

"Louise has asked me to play in your place on Saturday. I know you suggested it to her, too. Well, my chance has come and I am miserably unhappy at the very thought. I know I'll make a million fouls and we'll lose the game. Darn every bedroom slipper that was ever invented!

"Your doleful,
"Betty."

"Poor old Bet," smiled Polly. "Well, if she only makes good I won't be half so unhappy at not playing myself."

In less than five minutes she was sound asleep, and the next morning Miss King pronounced her temperature normal.

CHAPTER XII—POLLY'S HEROISM

"Miss King, don't you think I might be carried to the game tonight?" pleaded Polly early Saturday morning as the nurse was bathing her face and hands.

"We'll see; perhaps we can arrange it if you have no fever," answered Miss King, and Polly had to be content.

After study hour Lois and Betty flew up to the infirmary.

"Everything's going beautifully," announced Lois excitedly, "and we brought you up the green and white ribbons; here, let me tie them on your arm."

"How's the ankle? Do you think you can get over to the game?" asked Betty eagerly.

"If I have no fever, Miss King says she'll see. I hate people to say they will see; Aunt Hannah always did, and it always meant 'no,'" pouted Polly. "When does the other team arrive?"

"The train's due at 12:03, luncheon at 12:30, and the game's called for 2 o'clock," Lois told her.

Just then Angela and Connie appeared in the doorway.

"May we come in? How's the invalid?" Connie asked.

"Oh, hello. Of course come in. I'm awfully glad to see you. I am feeling very fine this morning," responded Polly.

Angela was looking dolefully at the big lump the bandaged foot made under the covers, and her eyes were misty.

"Polly," she began, "can you ever forgive—"

"Angela, you're going to say something about those slippers, and if you do—" Polly interrupted threateningly.

"All right, I won't, but I'll think of it for the rest of my life."

After a few minutes of excited conversation the girls left—Lois and Betty for the gym and Angela and Connie for the schoolroom to practice songs with the rest.

Polly, left alone, retied and patted the green and white ribbon Lois had given her; then she tossed and turned and fretted until the doctor arrived an hour later. He declared the ankle greatly improved, but he did not like the patient's nervous condition, and to Polly's plea to be carried to the gym, he gave a decided "No."

Miss King was all sympathy, and offered to read aloud, tell stories, or, in fact, do anything to amuse her heartbroken little patient, but Polly refused to be comforted.

After luncheon Lois and Betty arrived for a last word; they were in their gym suits and Betty's hands were ice cold. Polly tried to be encouraging and cheerful.

"Do be careful of those lines, Bet," she advised, "and don't run with the ball."

"Run with the ball! I probably won't have a chance to even get my hands on it let alone run with it. Oh, I tell you, I'm in a sweet funk!" groaned Betty.

"Will you stop talking like that, Betty Thompson," commanded Lois. "You ought to be ashamed of yourself. Why, if you can't play against that insignificant Whitehead center, all my little faith in man is gone."

"Do tell me something about the other team," Polly begged. "I heard you giving them the cheer as they arrived. Do they look very dreadful?"

"No, I think we are pretty evenly matched. Their guards are tall—but there goes the bell; we'll have to fly. Polly, darling, I'll come and tell you all about it the second the game's over," promised Lois, as she and Betty ran down to the schoolroom to join the team.

As Polly lay listening she heard the girls tramping over to the gym. The sound came faintly at first, then louder, and finally halted underneath the infirmary window:

"Oh, there is a girl who's known in these parts.
Her name is Polly Pendleton, and she's won our hearts!
Oh, we'd like to know a girl with more go,
And we will stand by her to the end—O!"

sang fifty voices, and then the tramping started once more and grew fainter as the girls neared the gym.

Poor Polly buried her head in the pillow and sobbed:

"To think of my having a chance to play in the big game and then not being able to! Why, I can't even watch it!" she cried. "Why didn't I see those hateful steps?"

Miss King came in and asked if there was anything she could do.

"I am quite at your service," she assured her.

"Do you really mean that?" answered Polly. "Then go over to the gym and watch the game for a little while and come back and tell me how it's going, and if we have a chance. I promise to be good," she added.

Miss King thought it over and decided to go. It would please her unhappy patient, and besides she loved to see a good game herself.

"I won't stay very long," she said. "If you want anything you can reach the bell that rings in the other house."

"Don't come back unless we are winning," called Polly as she watched the white nurse's cap disappear down the long flight of steps that led from the infirmary to the ground. They had been built so that if there were any contagious cases in the infirmary, the girls could reach the grounds without going into any other part of the buildings.

Then, tired from the excitement of the day, she sank back in the pillows to rest until Miss King's return. She dozed off to sleep for about fifteen minutes, and when she next opened her eyes she was conscious of the smell of smoke.

She raised herself on her elbow and looked out of the dormer window beside her bed. From there she could see the Bridge of Sighs which, as you know, connected the two buildings of the school. A thin spiral of smoke was pouring out from the top of the middle window.

Her first thought was the bell. She rang it violently, but with no success, for the maids were in the laundry gossiping over a cup of tea, and the bell clanged to an empty kitchen.

Something had to be done and Polly realized that that something rested with her. As quickly as her ankle would permit—it was, of course, paining her terribly—she got into such of her clothes as she could find in the infirmary, threw Miss King's cape around her, and thrust her stockinged feet once again into Angela's Chinese slippers.

"Now," she thought, as she limped painfully down the steps, "the thing to do is to get one of the teachers' attention without letting the girls know anything is wrong."

The fifty feet to the gym seemed as many miles to Polly. At first the excitement of her errand kept her up, but as she neared the gym the burning pain in her ankle forced her to stop every few feet to rest.

When at last she stumbled up the steps of the gym, she was met at the door by Mrs. Baird and Miss King, who were just leaving.

"Polly, what is it?" gasped both women, hurrying to her side.

"The Bridge of Sighs is on fire—no one answered the bell—I had to come— don't tell the girls!" And Polly, her message delivered, fainted dead away in Miss King's arms and was carried back unconscious to the infirmary.

The fire was soon under control. Mrs. Baird called the stablemen, and together with the fire extinguishers it was over almost at once. It had started by two wires crossing and, fortunately, on the bridge. It might easily have spread to both buildings had it not been for Polly's timely warning. So quietly and quickly had it happened that the girls in the gym knew nothing of it.

When Polly next opened her eyes, Mrs. Baird and Miss King were standing on either side of her bed.

"Is it out?" she asked, turning to Mrs. Baird.

"Yes, dear, it is; thanks to you and your splendid courage," Mrs. Baird replied, taking her hand in hers and patting it.

"And the game?" demanded Polly, now thoroughly conscious. "Is it over?"

A prolonged shout from the gym answered her question.

"It must be just over," explained Miss King, "and that shout sounds as if we had won. How is the ankle, dear? Very painful?"

"Yes, it is kind of sore," Polly admitted, "but I want to know the score," she insisted.

Mrs. Baird gave her hand a tight squeeze and smiled down at her as she answered:

"I'll go this minute and find out; they are probably waiting for me to present the cup. I will send you the score at once," she promised as she left the room.

Seddon Hall had made a hard fight and when the time was up the score on the board was 10 to 8 in their favor. Betty had surprised everybody by her good work. She had not given the other center a chance at the ball and she had made only one foul. Perhaps the thought of Polly waiting anxiously in the infirmary for news of the game had spurred her on. Before the game started she had said to Lois:

"I may be in a blue funk, but won this game shall be, if I have anything to say about it. Polly shan't be disappointed."

And Betty had kept her word. She had managed the passes so well that Louise, who at the beginning of the game had been in a fever of apprehension, had almost wept with joy.

As Mrs. Baird entered they were cheering the losing team. With a few well-chosen words of congratulations, she presented the cup to Louise Preston, and finished with a brief account of the fire and the part Polly had played in it.

Useless to try to describe the girls' enthusiasm; they cheered and cheered. Mrs. Baird dispatched Lois and Betty to tell Polly the score, and the rest of the girls stood under the infirmary window and sang to her until their throats were hoarse.

Betty and Lois, still in their gym suits, sat on the end of her bed and told her all about the game.

"Betty, darling, if you were not so hot and dirty I think I could eat you," Polly exclaimed. "Think of your making only one little foul. Oh, but I'm proud of you!"

"Well, you see, you told Louise to put me on the team in your place," Betty explained, "and I had to make good."

Polly turned to Lois:

"I am awfully sorry you didn't get a chance to play," she said.

"I'm kind of glad," Lois replied. "Now, perhaps, we will both play on Field Day."

"Here, here, what are you daring to suggest?" demanded Louise Preston from the doorway. She was followed by the rest of the team. They had waited to see the Whitehead girls off and then changed from their gym suits before coming to see the heroine of the day.

"Oh, I was only hoping a couple of you big team girls would give us subs a chance on Field Day. You are dreadfully selfish, you know," Lois replied.

Polly smiled happily at her captain.

"Well, you did win the game without me, Louise, didn't you?" she asked.

"How do you make that out?" Florence Guile demanded. "I think you had a pretty big hand in it. If you hadn't been so plucky and kept so still about the fire, we'd have all been frightened to death and the game never would have been even finished."

"Florence is right," agreed everybody. "Three long cheers for plucky Polly!"

"To the victor belongs the spoils," laughed Louise. When the girls had stopped cheering: "Here's the cup. I brought it up to show you, and you may keep it as long as you like."

Polly took it reverently in her hands and looked at it for a long time. Finally she said:

"What a funny day it's been. Please don't any one talk any more about the fire. I'm sick of it, and besides it was the game that counted." Then as she caught sight of Angela among the crowd of girls at the door she said:

"Come here, Angela. I have something to tell you, you must apologize to your slippers; they have atoned for their crime; they carried me safely all the way to the gym."

Miss King appeared at the door as the girls were laughing at Polly's remark.

"Is this a reception by any chance?" she inquired. "I'm sorry to interrupt, but you'll all have to leave. Polly's supper is on its way from the kitchen and I'm sure she doesn't want an audience while she is eating it."

The girls left after more congratulations and promises to come back the first thing next day, and Polly was left alone to gaze happily at the big silver loving cup which, in a measure, she had helped win for Seddon Hall.

CHAPTER XIII—BETTY'S IDEA

The long days in the infirmary dragged by and lengthened into weeks. One so closely resembled the other that Polly lost track of all time. Uncle Roddy sent boxes containing everything that his generous mind could think of, to amuse the invalid, and the girls did their best to make the days fly.

At last the time came when, with the aid of a crutch and Miss King, Polly managed to hobble down the steps and out into the sunshine. It was only a matter of a couple of weeks after that, that she discarded the crutch, and on a never-to-be-forgotten day made her appearance, a little worn and shaky still, at the beginning of the Literature class. No one expected her, and her welcome was all that she could have dreamed of.

In the meantime the snow had melted, to be replaced by slush and, as March ended, by mud. Polly slipped back easily into her accustomed place. Easter vacation, spent at Atlantic City with Uncle Roddy, came and went, so that when this chapter opens, spring was fully established and Seddon Hall was a mass of dogwood and violets.

Today was the day of the Faculty tea, to be given by the Seniors, and Polly, Lois, and Betty were helping them make the sandwiches and fruit punch.

"Wah, but I'm hot and tired!" sighed Lois, holding a thin slice of bread in one hand and a knife smeared with mayonnaise dressing in the other.

"You're lazy, you mean," replied Betty. "Try squeezing a few of these lemons if you want a sample of real work; they're as hard as rocks."

Polly looked up, flushed from her task.

"I've an idea," she exclaimed. "Look! Put the lemon on the floor and roll it gently with your toe. See how soft it gets!" she continued as she cut the rolled lemon in half and squeezed out the juice.

"Bright idea!" congratulated Betty. "Why didn't you think of it before?" And putting a lemon on the floor, she started rolling it vigorously.

"Lo, if you could see how funny you look," she added. "You've a daub of dressing on the end of your nose."

"Oh, would some power the giftie gie us, to see ourselves as others see us," quoted Lois. "Who said that?" she inquired.

(Please remember Betty was still rolling the lemon).

One of the Sophomores, busy at the other end of the table, caught the remark and, to tease Betty who was renowned for her knowledge of quotations, called:

"Sir Thomas Moore, didn't he?"

"Moore!" yelled Betty. "Certainly not! Robert Burns wrote it. Such ignorance! I am surprised!"

Some one else exclaimed: "Why, Betty, you are crazy. Burns never said anything as clever as that."

Poor Betty was all up in arms. Like most people that love to tease, she was not always conscious when she was being teased herself.

"He didn't, didn't he?" she demanded. "Well, I'll *prove* to you that he did."

At the word prove, delivered in her most emphatic manner, she put so much extra pressure on the poor long-suffering lemon that it gave a prolonged squashy noise and oozed out all over the floor.

"Oh, Bet, what a mess!" exclaimed Polly. "Look at the floor!"

Betty looked and grumbled disgustedly:

"That ends it. I'll squeeze no more lemons. It's all your fault, anyhow, Polly, for telling me to step on them."

"Excuse me, dear," said Polly meekly, "I meant with moderation."

As the girls stood laughing around the remains of the lemon, Louise Preston entered the room.

"I can't get any one to pick violets for me. We've only one bowlful and we need loads." Then as she saw the floor she asked: "Who's been throwing lemons?"

"Oh, Bet got mad because I put a quotation in Moore's mouth that belonged to Burns, her beloved," laughed Mary Right.

"Well, suppose you three girls go and get us some more flowers," suggested Louise. "You don't look as if you were enjoying this very much and, besides, we can't waste lemons."

"We will go with pleasure," chorused the three.

"Thanks ever so much," said Louise, and she added as they were leaving the room: "Please don't do any arguing while you're about it, or Bet may step on the violets."

Ten minutes later the three were making their way to a brook whose banks they knew would be covered with long-stemmed dogtooth violets.

"Ungrateful wretches, these Seniors," grunted Betty, seating herself on a rock and stretching. "Work your fingers to the bone and never even get asked to come in the back door to their party."

"Seems to me," mused Polly, "that all the other classes do the entertaining and the Freshmen do all the work."

They were still for a few minutes and sat lazily on the moss watching the water gurgle over the stones at the bottom of the brook. Finally Betty exclaimed:

"I have it, the best idea! Listen! Why don't we give a farewell party to the Seniors?"

"It's never been done," replied Lois.

"What of that? There's got to be a first time to everything, and it would be such a lark."

"But what kind of a party?"

"A moonlight straw-ride and supper at Flat Rock," suggested Polly. "Mrs. Baird would let us, I know, she's such a dear."

"How about the other girls?" inquired Lois. "Angela and Connie would love it, of course, but the rest—"

"The rest don't count," cut in Betty. "We have the majority and, besides, they always do what we suggest."

"Let's call a class meeting tonight," said Polly. "And now, if we don't start to gather some violets, the Seniors won't accept our invitation if we do ask them to a party."

For an hour they picked flowers and discussed the plans.

"None of your garden parties with ice-cream and cake for me; there's never any fun in that," remarked Betty, dipping a handful of withered violets into the brook.

"Besides, that is what the 'sofs' have planned to do. Mary Rice told me about it, confidentially," added Lois.

"Therefore you immediately tell us," laughed Betty. "Well, they need not be afraid of our copying them. Polly's plan's the best, if we can only do it."

"Listen!" commanded Polly. "Wasn't that some one calling up there?"

"Hello!" called a voice directly above them.

The girls looked and there, standing on a rock, were Connie and Angela, with their arms full of dogwood.

"Come on down," sang out Betty. "You're just the ones we want; we've a wonderful idea."

"Great! Bully!" exclaimed Angela and Connie when they had heard the plan. "Why didn't any one ever think of it before?"

"We can take bacon in jars, and rolls, and broil the bacon over a regular camp fire," suggested Connie.

"And I'll make up a new song just to the Seniors. None of the other classes have ever done that," announced Angela.

"If we don't hurry back the Seniors will think we're lost," reminded Polly. Then with a sigh she added: "I do hope the rest of the class will like the idea."

They did. A class meeting was called and everybody voted it a dandy plan. The two Dorothys said their only objection would be in case the Spartan were chosen for chaperone. The rest laughed at the very thought and Polly promised to annihilate the first one to make such a horrible suggestion.

Lois was chosen to ask Mrs. Baird, and returned from the office with her full permission.

The day was set for the following Friday night, and Angela was told to write a song.

In the corridor that evening as the girls were talking over the plans for the party, one of the maids appeared with a covered tray.

"From the Seniors," she explained, handing it to Lois. "For Miss Polly, Miss Betty, Miss Angela, Miss Connie, and you."

"Food!" exclaimed Betty. "Why, the Seniors aren't such ungrateful wretches as I thought them."

"Indeed they are not; they've the best class in the school," protested Lois.

"With one exception," Polly corrected, "the Freshmen."

And after a subdued cheer they started in to make short work of the tray's contents.

CHAPTER XIV—THE FRESHMEN ENTERTAIN

Friday arrived, clear and sunshiny, with just enough chill in the air to make sweaters comfortable.

The Freshmen class were so excited that they found it impossible to pay any attention in classes. The teachers, for the most part, understood and forgave, except the Spartan, who was, of course, more trying than usual.

After the last bell the Freshmen met in one of the classrooms to decide about the last details. Although they had no class officers, it was almost always Lois who acted as president at all their meetings. Such was the case today.

"Everybody stop talking for one second," she commanded, swinging herself to the top of the desk. "The first thing to think about is food," she continued, as the girls dropped into chairs, and there was a lull in the conversation.

Betty jumped up, announcing emphatically:

"You may count me out on that; no more squashed lemons for little Betty."

"There's not much to get ready," Polly remarked. "There's the rolls and bacon—they're ordered—and the ginger pop, the potato chips, and the apples and bananas are here. There's really nothing to make but the Boston brown bread sandwiches. Who'll make them?" And she looked questioningly at the two Dorothys.

"We will," volunteered one of them. "What goes in between—cream cheese and grape jelly?"

"Yes," answered Betty, "and for goodness' sake, Dot, don't get original and put anything else in on your own hook."

"Betty, do be serious for once," pleaded Lois. "There's loads to be done. Have you finished the song, Angela?"

"Yes, and I say we wait until we've finished supper and are all sitting around the fire before we sing it to them," suggested Angela.

Everybody agreed that that was a good idea.

"It's to the tune of 'There is a Tavern Near the Town,' isn't it?" asked Roberta Andrews. "I haven't learned the words yet."

"Oh," Lois interrupted, jumping down from the desk, "we forgot all about the straw for the wagon. Berta, will you and Ruth see to that? MacDonald said we could have as much as we wanted if we'd go to the stable and get it."

"All right, that will be a lark," agreed Berta. "Come on, Ruth, we'd better get right at it now." And the two girls, after parting instructions from Lois, left for the stable.

"If we are going to make those sandwiches," began Dot Mead, "we'd better go, too."

"Righto!" agreed her twin in name, and together they started for the kitchen.

"And now what are you going to do with me, Ruler of the Universe?" inquired Connie.

Lois looked at her for a minute and then replied:

"I think you and Angela might go out and cut sticks to broil the bacon on."

"Cut their fingers off, you mean. Certainly not," exploded Betty. "They may find the sticks, but I will do the whittling."

And taking Connie and Angela each by an arm, Betty escorted them out of the room.

When Lois and Polly were left alone, they hugged each other joyously.

"And now for the express-room," Polly whispered mysteriously.

At five o'clock the big farm wagon, filled with hay and drawn by two big gray horses, was waiting in the driveway under the Bridge of Sighs.

"Everything in?" shouted Angela. "Steamer rugs and food?"

"Yes, all in," answered Betty, who was patting the horses' noses.

Polly and Lois were standing just around the corner of the house and out of sight of the other girls.

"Now's the time to get it in," whispered the latter. She used the same mysterious tone of voice in which Polly had spoken of the express-room earlier in the day.

A few minutes later, under the hurry and excitement of starting, they smuggled a large box, unnoticed, under the driver's seat.

"Safe and sound, and nobody saw," Lois whispered softly. "Every one in?" she called out. "All aboard."

The Seniors were each seated beside a Freshman, Louise Preston was between Lois and Polly. Miss Stuart and Miss Porter, who were chaperoning the party, sat beside the driver, where all good chaperons ought to sit.

As the barge rolled out of the school grounds, the girls sang the favorite Seddon Hall song, which ended in the words:

"It's the only school in the wide, wide world."

At first, things were a little dull. There was a big distance between the oldest and youngest classes of the upper school, but after a while the Seniors forgot their dignity and the Freshmen their respect.

When Flat Rock, a huge boulder with a table top, overlooking a small lake, was reached, everybody was in the best of spirits, and they piled out and helped unload.

Polly and Lois, as before, captured the mysterious box and managed to hide it in the bushes. A camp fire, under Miss Stuart's direction, was soon blazing, and the girls were seated on rugs and pillows, toasting bacon.

Now every one knows that a bacon bat is loads of fun to talk about before it happens, and to remember afterwards, but the actual eating of the bacon, which is always burned long before it is cooked, is not so much fun in itself.

This bacon bat was like every other. When the bacon was all gone, and a good deal of it had been surreptitiously thrown away, every one looked around for something to really eat. The sandwiches were not very satisfying, and it was too soon to offer the bananas.

The Freshmen began to look uneasy. It entered their heads that perhaps their party was not going to be the success they had planned. Then just as Polly and Lois were exchanging glances, Betty, who was hunting for more wood for the fire, stumbled over the mysterious box.

67

"Hello, what's this?" she called. "Why, it says Freshman Class on it."

Every one pounced on the box and opened it, to find a big fat turkey all carved but held together by a narrow white ribbon, paper plates and napkins and drinking cups, cranberry jelly, a huge chocolate cake, any quantity of cookies, and boxes of candy.

Well, you can imagine the surprise. As each new item was unpacked, there was a chorus of exclamations, such as:

"Where under the sun did it come from?"

"Do look at the immense turkey!"

"Somebody knew I loved home-made cookies!"

"Please, all, leave me alone with this chocolate cake!"

No one knew where it came from except Betty, who caught on at once, and Polly and Lois made her keep still. It was a royal spread, which means everybody ate more than was good for them.

When it was finally over and they were all sitting comfortably around the fire, the Freshmen started singing Angela's song:

```
"There is a flat rock near the school, near the
school,
Where we abandon every rule, every rule,
And mingle with the Seniors fair
And never, never think of care!

You're the oldest class of all the year, all the
year,
And we're the very youngest here, youngest here,
Three years will pass and we'll be Seniors, too,
And we're going to try to be like you!

Fare thee well, for we must leave you,
Do not let this parting grieve you,
But remember that the best of friends must part,
Adieu, dear Seniors fair, adieu, adieu, adieu,
We can no longer stay with you, stay with you,
Three rousing cheers for the class of '15,
They are the best we've ever seen!"
```

(Angela never was satisfied with the last line.) Louise Preston was sitting with Lois and Polly on either side of her, and as the song ended, she put her arm around each of them.

"This has been the very best party of the whole year," she said, "and I think I know something about the way the wonderful box came to be here."

Polly and Lois tried to appear very innocent, but it was of no use. Finally Polly said:

"Well, perhaps you do, but please don't tell any one what you know."

"All right, I promise," Louise said, "but I will tell *you* two this much—you're quite the sweetest children in the school, and I can't tell you how much I and the rest of the Seniors appreciate all the things you have done for us this year."

"I'll tell you how you can—" laughed Lois "—by letting us help some more."

It was now the Seniors' turn to cheer, and they did it most heartily, calling each Freshman's name in turn. Then Betty, who was very full of turkey and bananas, got up to make a speech.

"'Friends, Romans and Countrymen,'" she began, "lend me your ears." Then mimicking the chaplain, she continued: "My dear young friends, tonight has been one of the pleasures never to be forgotten. The bacon was perhaps not all that it might have been, but surely we can afford to overlook that in the face of this blessed turkey."

"Somebody throw something at Betty; she's off," Angela called.

"Come and help reload," suggested Connie.

With a few muttered remarks about an unappreciative audience, Betty brought her speech to a laughing close and turned to, with a will, to replace the rugs and pillows. In a short time everything was in, and the wagon started for home.

It was a glorious ride. The Freshmen repeated their song and cheered and cheered the Seniors, and the Seniors returned the compliment.

When there was a lull in the singing, as they passed through the village, Betty, almost asleep in the hay, grunted:

"You may all thank me for this party; it never would have happened if I hadn't squashed that bally lemon."

The wagon drew up under the Bridge of Sighs, just as the big school clock tolled ten o'clock. The girls parted with many thanks on both sides, and they were all conscious that they would remember this as the jolliest evening of the year.

As Polly and Lois said good night in the latter's room, Lois said:

"Well, it was a success, and no one but Bet and Louise guessed about the box."

"Wasn't it!" agreed Polly. "I'm awfully glad we thought of it; we'd have starved if we hadn't. I think the Seniors enjoyed it, too. Isn't Louise a darling? Do you know, Lo, if I wasn't so strongly opposed to 'crushes,' I might get an awful one on Louise."

"Could you?" smiled Lois in reply. "I'll tell you a secret—I've had quite a desperate one on her myself for two years."

Later, as Polly slipped into bed, she said aloud to the pictures on the wall:

"What a wonderful box it was." And closing her eyes she murmured sleepily: "Bless Uncle Roddy's heart."

CHAPTER XV—VISITORS

Lois bounded up the stairs, two steps at a time, waving a yellow telegram in the air and shrieking: "Polly!" at the top of her lungs. Not finding her friend in the corridor, she started for the gym, and discovered her there vigorously bouncing the basket-ball.

"Polly, come here quick," she cried; "I've just had a wire from Dad saying he, mother and Bob are coming up here this afternoon."

Polly tucked the ball under one arm and put the other on Lois' shoulder.

"Are they really?" she asked delightedly. "What time?"

"The wire doesn't tell, just says, this afternoon. They may be here any minute." Then rubbing her cheek against Polly's she added, coaxingly:

"You'll help me entertain them won't you, Poll, and stay with us all the time they're here? Promise."

Polly made a wild attempt to throw the ball in the basket, half way across the room as she answered:

"Of course I will, what do you want me to do?"

"Hurry and get out of your suit first," said Lois. "I'm going to ask Mrs. Baird about the trains."

Polly hurried to her room to change, and was just tying her sailor tie, when Lois knocked at the door.

"They can't get here until three thirty," she announced. "So there's loads of time."

Polly had almost completed her dressing.

"What are you going to do with them?" she asked, giving a vigorous, last brush to her wavy hair and straightening her bows.

"They've seen the grounds, haven't they?"

"Bob never has," Lois answered. Then, after a minute of thoughtful silence:

"Polly, what are we going to do with them? Mother and Father are all right but Bob's sure to do something awful, he's such a tease."

"Oh, don't worry about him," laughed Polly; "if the worst comes to the worst, you can take him out of bounds."

In spite of this suggestion, Lois' brows remained puckered and her expression worried. She was not thinking so much about how to amuse Bob. She was wondering how, now that these two were at last to meet, they would like each other. Suppose they didn't like each other at all! Dreadful thought; Polly might think Bob too grown up and quiet, and Bob might think her "a silly girl." Lois looked forlorn when she contemplated such an outcome to this meeting.

She still wore a puzzled expression as she waited on the steps a little later, watching for the first sign of the Station Carriage. At three o'clock it came in sight around the first bend of the road. When it reached the porte-cochère, her father was the first to get out and he almost smothered Lois in his big hug.

Big, was the word that described Dr. Farwell, everything about him was big. His broad shoulders, his well shaped hands, his kindly deep set blue eyes, even his voice, which appeared to come from his boots as he asked:

"How is this little daughter of mine?"

"Oh, Daddie, dear, I'm so glad to see you. I'm perfectly fine," Lois answered excitedly and then turned to greet her mother.

"Darling Lois," Mrs. Farwell whispered, kissing her, and:

"Sweetheart mother," Lois whispered back. That was all. Mother and daughter understood each other so well, that there was no need for words.

"Well, don't I get even a how d'ye do?" demanded a laughing voice. And a big hand fell on Lois' shoulder.

"Why, Bobbie—but of course you do, I'm so glad to see you, I could eat you up," she cried.

"Eat this instead, won't you?" said Bob, producing a big white cardboard box. "It's a chocolate cake—it won't be quite so tough. Heppy made it for you, and she said she 'sho' did hope her baby chile would like it.'"

"Bless Heppy's heart, she's a darling, give me the box, you're sure to drop it."

"I like that, after I've carried it all the way here. I've a good mind to feed it to the horse," Bob threatened.

"Hadn't you better take us to the reception-room, dear?" Mrs. Farwell reminded. "We want to say how do you do to Mrs. Baird."

Lois led, dancing every step of the way. At the door of the room she pointed to a cozy group of chairs in the corner. "You wait here," she said, "and I'll go tell her; she's always in her office at this time."

"Thank you, dear, and oh, can't we meet Polly?" asked her mother and Dr. Farwell added:

"Yes, of course we must meet Roddy's niece."

Lois called back, "I'll get her first, I have Mrs. Baird's permission." And disappeared down the corridor. On reaching Freshman Lane she knocked at Polly's door.

"Polly, they're here, hurry up."

"Wait a minute, I'm changing my shoes," Polly answered.

But she did not add, for the fourth time:

"Whatever for?"

"Oh, my others needed a shine."

"Well, hurry up, do. When you're ready come down to the reception hall. I'll meet you."

And Lois was off again, but instead of returning to her family, she suddenly remembered Mrs. Baird, and went off in search of her.

When Polly reached the reception-room, after deciding the weighty question of shoes, she found Bobbie, all six feet of him, blocking the doorway.

He was standing with his hands behind him, his head thrown back, and his eyes fixed intently on a colored print of Venice that hung to the right of the door.

Dr. Farwell was hidden by the piano. Farther back in the room Mrs. Farwell was looking out of the window and smiling. She had thrown back her dark brown feather boa, that so nearly matched her eyes, and Polly could see a waterfall of soft cream lace at her neck; her hands were in her lap, and she tapped the floor with one ridiculously tiny foot.

As Polly slowly approached the door she thought, wistfully, "What a darling to have for a mother," and then, "how under the sun will I ever get past Bob. Well, I'm here now and I can't run." And taking her courage in both hands, she walked the rest of the way to the door, and after a nervous little cough, said:

"I beg your pardon."

Bob, startled from his reverie, turned, and seeing her, jumped to one side.

"Oh, I'm sorry! excuse me, I—" In his confusion he backed into the piano stool and sat down suddenly without meaning to.

At the sound, Doctor and Mrs. Farwell both looked up, and the Doctor said:

"Why, Bob, what—?" and then laughed.

Mrs. Farwell took in the situation at a glance, and went over to Polly, who was blushing violently, with outstretched hand.

"I'm sure you must be Polly," she said. "Lois has written me so much about you, that I know I can't be mistaken."

"How do you do, Mrs. Farwell?" Polly answered shyly. "I am Polly. Lois said to come down, that she'd be here."

"She's looking for Mrs. Baird," Mrs. Farwell explained.

"Do let me present my husband to you."

"So this is Polly?" said the Doctor. "I am delighted to see you, my dear. I used to know Roddy well. You and he were so good to Lois Christmas vacation that I don't know how to thank you enough."

"And this is my son, Bob," Mrs. Farwell continued, without giving Polly a chance to reply.

Bob held out a big hand,

"How do you do Miss Pendleton?"

"How do you do, Mr. Farwell?"

They said together, and then both fell into a confused silence.

Fortunately, Lois entered at that moment.

"Oh, there you are, Polly," she said. "Mrs. Baird will be here right away, mother. You and Dad stay here and talk to her, and Polly and I will take Bob for a walk, and show him the grounds."

The two girls ran up stairs for their sweaters, and in a jiffy they were leading Bob towards the gym.

At first, Lois did most of the talking, for Polly and Bob were very quiet.

The one was thinking: "If Lo had been there I would not have been so embarrassed."

And the other: "Of all the brilliant ways of meeting a girl, falling over a chair is the best! I am the Clumsiest, etc., etc."

But as they entered the gym Polly forgot her shyness, and as she rattled on about basket-ball and the coming Field Day, Bob was able to console his injured pride with the thought that after all, she was only one of his kid sister's friends.

In the course of their walk, which led them past all the landmarks in the grounds, they talked to each other with the ease of old friends, and Bob had started to tease.

"Lois says you play basket-ball wonderfully," he said to Polly, as they tramped through the woods on their way to the old fort.

"I don't play half as well as she does," she answered. "Besides, she knows nothing about it; I've never played in a big game. Perhaps if I did, I'd lose my nerve."

"You almost played once," Lois reminded her.

"What happened?"

"I sprained my ankle instead."

"Oh, was that the time you were so plucky about giving the fire alarm? That was great; Lo wrote me about it."

"What else could I have done? I couldn't very well let the place burn down, could I?" Polly asked, smiling a little self-consciously.

"I suppose not," Bob said aloud. Adding to himself, "For a girl as young as she is, she's remarkably sensible."

They walked on in silence, taking long swinging strides.

The thump, thump of their footsteps echoed and reëchoed in the silent woods. They reached the top of Fort Hill and stopped for a minute to get their breath. The wind blew the girls' hair about their flushed faces and sent eddies of last fall's brown leaves swirling along the path before them.

Across the Hudson the sun was already half hidden by the hills. Below them the old stone fort sprawled half way down the steep slope that led to the river.

Bob's eyes rested on it inquiringly—"Hello, what have we here?" he asked.

"That's the old fort, built in the Revolution by the Americans to defend themselves against the attacking British," Lois recited, in a sing song voice. "It is said that at the brook we just crossed General George Washington once watered his horse while the founder of Seddon Hall held the bridle," she continued, smiling mischievously at her brother.

It was the tale that was told to all the new girls at school and there were always a few who believed it.

Bob laughed heartily.

"Come, Sis, that's too much, but you told it well. Why don't you add that Washington and his staff made the reception-room their headquarters?"

"I will the next time I tell it," Lois chuckled, pleased at the idea.

Polly had wandered off a little way down the slope, presently she called:

"Lo, do you remember the first time we came out here?"

"Yes, of course I do; we were getting greens for the Seniors. We talked so much we were nearly late for luncheon."

73

"Doesn't it seem ages ago? By the way, what time is it?"

Bob pulled out his watch.

"It's five, ten," he said.

"It's fate," exclaimed Polly; "we are always late when we come to the fort."

"Poor Mother and Dad, we'll have to hustle," said Lois.

They looked regretfully at the wonderful orange sky, turned, and with the wind at their backs, started off in the direction of the school.

Half an hour later, breathless from hurrying, they entered the reception-room and found Dr. and Mrs. Farwell still talking to Mrs. Baird, and lingering over the remains of their tea.

"Enjoyed your walk?" asked Mrs. Farwell.

"We've had such a cozy tea party that we haven't had time to miss you," the Doctor added.

Mrs. Baird acknowledged the compliment with a smile.

"If the girls are to go out to dinner," she said, "I think they had better go upstairs and dress: it's almost six o'clock."

"Are we going out to dinner?" exclaimed Lois.

"Yes, both of you," replied Mrs. Farwell; "so hurry up."

"Thank you so much, it's ever so kind of you to ask me, too," said Polly, suddenly mindful of Aunt Hannah and her instructions in manners, then, as suddenly forgetting them:

"What a lark, we'll be ready in a jiffy," and catching Lois by the arm she dragged her up stairs.

The Village hotel, under Dr. Farwell's insistent demands, produced a passably good dinner. Every one was in such high spirits that the time flew by.

"Isn't it funny," laughed Lois, as they delayed finishing their cream and cake, "to be having dinner here with my family? Last time it was with Uncle Roddy."

"Yes, isn't it?" agreed Polly. "I wonder what happened to the parrot?"

The waiter, who was passing the coffee, heard the question and said sadly:

"He died a month ago, Miss—of a cold in his head. We miss him sore," he added dolefully.

"What a shame!" exclaimed Polly and Lois together.

"I'll have to write Uncle Roddy and tell him," and Polly tried hard not to look amused.

The waiter looked grateful and after a polite "Thank you, Miss," left the room solemnly shaking his head.

The trouble with a good time is that there is always an end in sight. We often don't look for it, and then pretend it's not there. But we're sure to find it sooner or later lurking around the corner somewhere.

The end of this particular good time took the shape of the train to Albany, and the accusing hands of the hotel clock warned the Farwells of its near approach.

They saw the girls back to Seddon Hall and after repeated good-bys, drove off down the hill.

Polly and Lois watched the lamp on the carriage until it disappeared around a bend in the road.

"All over," sighed Lois, unwillingly coming back to earth. "And we missed study hour, and there's a Latin test tomorrow."

"Oh, bother Latin, we can get up early in the morning and cram. Lo, your mother and father are the dearest people I ever met. I mean it, truly," said Polly.

Lois looked at her intently. They were on the porch and it was dark—

"Don't you like Bob a little tiny bit, too?" she asked mischievously.

And Polly answered with provoking indifference:

"Why, of course."

CHAPTER XVI—GHOSTS

"Do you think you passed?" asked Betty, joining Angela and Polly in the schoolroom corridor. It was the third day of examination week and the Freshmen had just finished the Literature exam.

"I hope so," Polly answered. "It was awfully fair, don't you think?"

"Yes; but tell me one thing," Angela insisted, coming to a standstill and putting her hands on Betty's shoulder. "What did you say for the hint that Portia gave Bassanio about the caskets?"

"Why, the song—'Tell me where is fancy bred, in the heart or in the head?'" Betty answered.

"Don't you see" (Polly took up the explanation), "bred and head and all the other lines ended in a word that rimed with lead, and Portia hoped that Bassanio would think of that and choose the right casket."

"Too deep for me. I do remember, now, Miss Porter saying something about it, but I skipped that question," replied Angela. "Still, I think I passed."

They were on their way to Polly's room, but before they reached her door, Lois overtook them.

"Horrible news!" she announced. "Latin exam. this afternoon instead of tomorrow!"

"It can't be. How do you know?" demanded Betty.

"Saw it posted on the bulletin board."

"That woman's a fiend," Polly groaned. "I intended cramming this whole afternoon, and now what's to be done?"

"Anything particular you want to know?" Angela inquired. "Perhaps I can help you out a bit."

"No, there's no use; you'd have to begin from the very beginning," replied Polly, looking disconsolately out of the window at the glorious spring day.

Betty ruffled her hair and frowned.

"Something ought to be done to rile the Spartan," she said. "What shall it be?"

"She knows most of us will flunk," remarked Lois. "I suppose she'll be beastly sarcastic."

Angela, who had been curled up on the window seat and had apparently been paying no attention to the conversation, suddenly remarked:

"Give me a pencil, some one. I've an idea; it's not very clever, but it may annoy the Spartan."

"What is it?" they all demanded.

But Angela refused to tell. She got up, stretched lazily, and without a word to any one, left the room. In a few minutes she was back, wearing a thoroughly satisfied smile.

"Please tell us where you've been," teased Betty. "I'm bursting with curiosity."

"Why, I've been to the bulletin board. I wrote a little note to the Spartan."

That was quite enough for the girls. They flew over to the study hall corridor and crowded around the board. There at the end of the notice of the Latin examination, written in a big round hand, were the words:

"I came, I saw, I looked, I ran, I flew, I flunked!"

"Oh, that's too lovely for words!" gloated Lois. "Angela darling, I'll love you forever."

"Come on back to my room," urged Polly. "We don't want the Spartan to see us here; she'll know who did it."

"You're right; we had better fly. But O Jemima, wouldn't I love to watch her face when she first sees it!" chuckled Betty.

Once back in Polly's room the girls lapsed into silence and all opened Latin books, which doesn't mean, however, that they studied. Betty was wondering what particular chapter Miss Hale would choose for translation; Angela's thoughts were busy with a possible rhyme about the hard-heartedness of the Spartan, and Lois and Polly were thinking of the promised walk with Louise, which would have to be given up.

It was Connie who interrupted their thoughts by banging on the door.

"May I come in?" she called.

"Yes; we are all in the depths of despair, but you may come in if you want to," Polly called dolefully.

"Sweet fight going on in Senior Alley," Connie began after she had entered the room. "I've been down there ever since I came out of the exam, and I heard all about it."

"Well, for goodness' sake, tell us what's the matter," demanded Angela.

"Don't be impatient, I'm going to. Listen: Agnes Green," Connie commenced (Agnes was one of the Seniors and the kind of girl who always had a grudge against some one), "is furious at Louise; you know she always has disliked her because Lu didn't put her on the team. Well, it seems that the Senior class is divided as to whether or not they should wear white shoes on Commencement. Louise wants to and Agnes doesn't."

"Of course she doesn't," Polly interrupted angrily. "That girl would disagree with her own shadow! But go on."

"That's about all I know," resumed Connie. "Agnes railed at Louise; said she had always influenced the class the wrong way; was unfair, and I don't know what. When I left, Louise was in tears."

Connie stopped for breath and then began again.

"And here's another little bit of news, which will make you love Agnes some more: it seems that her brother and a friend of his from college are coming up here to see her tomorrow. You know the Latin examinations were fixed for then, so what does dear Agnes do but ask the Spartan to change the time so that she can chaperon her and brother and brother's friend on a nice long drive. Naturally the Spartan jumped at the idea and arranged to give all her exams this very afternoon. Now just what do you think of that?" she finished, flourishing her arms in the air.

The girls were speechless with rage. Finally Betty managed to say:

"Of course we knew about it; that's what we've been holding an indignation meeting over, but we didn't know whose fault it was."

"Well, you know it now," replied Connie, "and I know that I have to go and study; so long, everybody."

"I suppose I'd better, too," sighed Betty. "Come and help me, Angela. Jove! I hope it pours rain tomorrow and that Agnes and the Spartan both get drowned!" And Betty, having given vent to her feelings, left the room, taking Angela with her.

Lois and Polly, left alone, faced each other, all thoughts of Latin forgotten.

"What's to be done?" Polly demanded.

"I don't know," Lois answered. "We can't do much, but I would like Louise to know how we feel about it."

"We have time to pick her some violets and send them up to her before luncheon," Polly suggested.

"That's a good idea; she'll understand from that."

The violets were soon gathered and a willing Sophomore was found to deliver them.

When Lois and Polly saw the rest of their class again, they were at luncheon, and Lois asked:

"How did you get on with your cramming, Bet?"

"Oh, don't! My poor brain is in a dreadful whirl," groaned Betty. "But did you see the bulletin board?" she added.

"Why? Has the time for the exam been changed again?"

"No, but the Spartan has put up a new notice. Isn't that a scream?" And Betty chuckled gleefully.

"That is funny," agreed Lois, "but I do hope some of the girls saw Angela's note before it was taken down."

"They did all right; there was a crowd standing in front of it, howling with laughter, when the Spartan arrived. Dot Mead was there and she told me. Oh, the Spartan's in a sweet rage!" Betty assured them.

"Nothing to what she'll be in when she sees my paper," spoke up Connie. "Ah, me, we can't do more than flunk. If I could only have had this afternoon to study! Drat Agnes Green!"

Lois and Polly exchanged glances and the conversation changed to other subjects.

The much-talked-of and dreaded Latin exam, was not nearly so terrible after all. Although Miss Hale was a very disagreeable person, she was also a very good teacher, and the girls found the answers to the questions much more easily than they had expected.

Lois and Polly handed in their papers about the same time. A few minutes later they met in the corridor, and with a sigh of relief joined arms and sauntered off in the direction of their rooms. Polly said:

"Lois, I've an idea—about Agnes, I mean; I've been thinking it out all the time I was taking the exam, and I've thought of a plan."

"What is it?" questioned Lois. "I couldn't think of a thing except killing her, and that wouldn't do. Did you see Louise smile at us at luncheon? Bless her heart!"

"Yes, but listen," Polly insisted. "Here's my plan. Tonight, after the Senior 'lights out' bell, we are going down the fire escape and get on the roof of the porch. Agnes' room is the second from the end, and I happen to know she leaves her window down from the top. We will knock gently—"

"But she's sure to know it's some of the girls," interrupted Lois. "No one ever thinks of burglars up here."

"I don't want her to think of burglars," Polly replied solemnly. "I want her to think of ghosts."

"Oh, I see. We're going to play spooks. What a lark! But how are we to do it?"

"I haven't quite decided about the details, but I will before tonight. Lo, I'm going to give that girl the scare of her life!"

And Polly kept her word. That night at 10.15 the Seniors were awakened by a scream of terror from Agnes Green's room. She said she had seen a ghost. As the girls were trying to assure her, two figures in long capes were softly stealing back up the fire escape.

"I tell you it *was* ghosts!" Agnes insisted, in tears. "It had four arms, long white ones, and it waved them and moaned." And she covered her head with the blankets and shivered at the thought.

Upstairs the two figures had reached Lois' room.

"I hope she doesn't die of fright," whispered one.

"So do I, but I hope she's good and scared. That was a splendid idea of yours to wear those long-sleeved kimonos," answered the other.

"Good night," said the first, and slipped out to her own room.

"Good night," replied the second. "Louise and Latin are both avenged."

The next morning Agnes stayed in bed for breakfast, and the Seniors said she had had a nightmare, and it had made her very nervous.

Polly and Lois were rather heavy-eyed and kept exchanging glances.

Of course no one suspected them of having anything to do with Agnes' dream, that is, no one except Louise. She met them in the corridor after breakfast and whispered very softly:

"Thank you for my beautiful violets and 'the ghost.' I understood and I think you're both darlings!"

That was all they ever heard on the subject.

Agnes' brother and his friend arrived, and with the Spartan for chaperon, they went for a drive, but Agnes said she didn't enjoy it as much as she had expected to, she was so dreadfully upset.

CHAPTER XVII—POLLY INTERVENES

Polly had just washed her hair, and she was sitting on her shirt waist box before the open window drying it. It was a gloriously warm, sunshiny day and the twitter of birds, the spring smell of the earth and the lazy hellos of the girls as they greeted one another on the campus below, gave her a drowsy feeling of contentment. Exams were nearly all over, and every one seemed to be just waiting in happy anticipation of Commencement.

Except for a short talk by Mrs. Baird after dinner it was to be a free evening and the girls had been granted permission to stay out of doors until it was really dark. Mrs. Baird had said that now was the time to take a big deep breath before rushing into the coming week of excitement.

Polly, half asleep, felt the top of her head and found it nearly dry—she shifted her position to a half kneeling one, shook her hair over her face so that the sun might shine on the back of it, and cradling her head on her arm resumed her dreaming.

"I wonder where Lo is," she mused—"probably practicing in the gym with Bet. I wish I hadn't washed my hair. It seems awfully silly to waste this beautiful day just breathing. I wonder what we could do. Why doesn't Lo come up; she knows I can't go out. I believe I'm lonesome." Polly sat up as this thought took shape in her mind. "How absurd," she said aloud. And then she laughed. It was funny to think that after all the years she had spent alone that she could so soon forget how to amuse herself. It was the first time she had realized what a difference Seddon Hall had made to her.

"I'd better get used to it," she said again, but she looked very doleful at the prospect.

A few minutes later, as she was feeling sorry for herself, a rap sounded at the door and Lois' voice called:

"Oh, Poll, are you there?"

"Yes, come in."

"I've been looking all over the place for you."

"I told you I was going to wash my hair."

"Well, if you did I forgot it, and I've been all over the grounds trying to find you." Lois poked her head out of the window. "She's here, Bet, come on up," she called. "We have a plan for tonight," she continued; "it's too nice to waste time just roaming around."

"That's what I've been thinking. What are you going to do?"

Polly, now quite awake, was rubbing her head with the towel in an attempt to hurry the drying.

"Nothing very exciting, it's Bet's suggestion."

"I like that," Betty herself burst in upon them. "Not very exciting, just one of Betty's silly ideas." Lois and Polly laughed heartily. Nothing was quite so amusing as Betty trying to look offended.

"It's a perfectly good idea, Poll," Betty continued, "and fits in with this nice lazy day."

"What is it?"

"Just a walk to the fort after dinner. Of course when we get there, we can sing and—"

"Thrilling, Bet, thrilling," teased Lois, but Polly made her stop by pushing her down on the bed and stuffing a pillow over her mouth. To Betty she said:

"It's a bully idea. It ought to be wonderful near the river tonight. Who's going?"

Lois struggled under the pillow. "I'll be good, let me up," she pleaded. "Ugh! you nearly smothered me. I'll tell you who's going. We are, of course, and Ange and Connie, and the two Dorothys, because one of them can sing, and perhaps Florence and Louise and—oh, anybody else that wants to come along."

"Who'll chaperon?"

"Oh, I never thought of that."

"Let's ask Miss Porter; I know she'd like it." It was Polly's suggestion.

"Fine, she's just the one."

"Not if the two Dorothys come," Betty said decidedly. "Have you forgotten the row in class?"

"Then let's drop the two Dorothys," replied Lois.

"Wait, I've an idea," Polly exclaimed; "let's ask only the girls we like awfully well. We don't know when we'll ever be together again and—"

"Oh, Poll!" Lois protested. "Don't talk like that."

"Well, we don't know. Louise and Florence graduate; Connie may go to the conservatory, and Ange—"

"I see what you mean," Betty interrupted. "Make it a sort of farewell reunion and of course we'll take Miss Porter—she's our favorite teacher."

"It'll be worse than a funeral," Lois said dolefully, "but it's rather a pretty idea."

"Lo, stop being sentimental; let's get the girls," suggested Betty. "Poll, hurry up and fix your hair."

"It's still sopping."

"Never mind, stick it up any way. It's too warm to make any difference."

Later they stopped to consult on the "Bridge of Sighs." They had asked Angela and Connie, and Louise and Florence, and had left them delighted with the plan. Louise and Florence had a class meeting on, but they promised to come for a little while.

"Who else?" asked Betty, expectantly.

"I don't know," replied Polly; "I can't think of any one."

"Neither can I," Lois added, "except Miss Porter."

"Why, that's perfectly silly; don't tell me there are only four girls in school we like," protested Betty.

"You're forgetting ourselves," Lois reminded her.

"Yes, but even then."

"Let's each choose one other girl," suggested Polly. "Lo, you first, who do you want?"

Lois puckered her eyebrows and tried hard to think; finally she said, "I just don't want any one else and that's the truth."

Polly smiled, "Bet, it's your turn; who do you want?"

"Mine? All right, let's see. I like a lot of girls—there's you and Lois and Ange and Connie—and—Oh, Jemima, but you're all going and I can't think of any one else, can you?"

"No, I can't," Polly said, laughing, "so that's settled. Let's go and ask Miss Porter."

They found the English teacher in a perfect ocean of examination papers, a daub of red ink on one ear.

"Come in, girls, I suppose you want to know if you've passed," she said, smiling the welcome she always felt for this particular trio.

"Why, our papers aren't corrected are they?" Betty asked, excitedly. "I thought it would be days before we knew."

"Oh, please tell us," begged Polly.

"Not until I hear why you came," Miss Porter said.

"Oh, no, tell us our marks first, please, please, please," Lois beseeched.

"Very well, I will. I'm too delighted to keep it to myself another minute," Miss Porter's eyes snapped. "You all passed wonderfully well—I can't tell you your marks, that wouldn't be fair to the rest, but I am so proud of you all."

They accepted this unexpected good news with delight. Literature was more important to them than any other subject.

"Oh, great."

"Isn't that bully!"

"I was scared to death, the examination was so hard."

"Now tell me why you came." Miss Porter put down her pen and waited.

"Will you?"

"We thought—"

"Tonight—" They all began at once.

"It's your idea, Poll, go on," Lois said.

"Well," Polly began.

"Polly, Polly," Miss Porter chided, "all your wells will surely make an ocean and drown you some one of these days."

"Oh, I know it, but it's such an easy way to begin a sentence. I won't do it again." Polly took a long breath.

"You know tonight there is nothing to do, and we thought it would be nice to go for a walk, out to the fort, just we three, and Angela and Connie; Florence and Louise said they'd come for a little while if they could."

"Yes, and?" Miss Porter asked inquiringly.

"Oh, well, of course, we want you to come, too," Polly ended, rather lamely.

Miss Porter sat very still for a minute and then she smiled, and when Miss Porter smiled it was a rare treat. If you watched her long enough you always ended by smiling, too. "That is a jolly idea," she said, enthusiastically. "Of course I'll come. I can't think of any nicer way of spending this lovely evening." Then suddenly her face fell. "Oh, my dear children, I forgot."

"What?" they demanded.

"We haven't a free evening at all. We are to have a lecture."

"You mean Mrs. Baird? But she's only going to tell us the plans for next week; it won't take a minute," Betty said assuringly.

"No, that's not it; this is another quite unexpected lecture. Mrs. Baird told the faculty about it after luncheon, but it slipped my mind."

"Oh," Lois groaned, "what's it to be?"

"A lecture on New England during the Revolution, by Professor Hale."

"Hale? The Spartan—Miss Porter, did she have anything to do with it?" Betty's eyes flashed indignation.

"The Professor is Miss Hale's cousin, I believe, and she was responsible for his coming. I think the lecture will be a very interesting one. He is going to show pictures." Miss Porter tried to be cheerful.

"Lantern slides?" demanded Polly.

"Yes, I believe that's it. I'm sorry about the walk, it would have been so nice." Miss Porter looked wistfully out of the window, as if she could see the old fort bathed in moonlight that very second. "But I am sure we will enjoy the lecture," she added hastily. The girls knew that no matter how strongly Miss Porter sympathized with them she would not permit a word against Miss Hale.

They left in silence and waited until they were in Polly's room, with the door closed, before they gave vent to their feelings.

Lois threw herself on the bed in despair. "If that isn't the meanest thing I ever heard of."

"To have to stay in on an evening like this and listen to History," Betty raged.

"History and the Spartan's cousin," Lois, cross as she was, could not help laughing at the combination.

"I suppose it's to get even; we weren't awfully pleasant about the Latin exam." Betty was jumping at conclusions.

"Oh, Bet, how silly." Polly turned from her place at the window. "The Spartan's not as bad as all that, she probably thinks we'll enjoy it."

"Yes, she does," Betty was skeptical.

"Polly, talk sense," Lois begged. "How could any one think that we'd rather listen to—Oh, mercy, when I think of it—the Revolution, battles and dates—Maybe the Spartan means well, only—"

But Polly was again looking out of the window. Her eye traveled over the familiar objects. The tennis court, the gym roof, and a little farther on, the corner of the stables and the power house. Something in the queer shaped little stone building caught her attention.

Betty was still raving. "But Lo, that's not the worst of it, we'll have to look at millions and hundreds of postal cards, while the Spartan's cousin explains them like this:

"My dear young ladies," Betty snatched up a nail file from Polly's dresser and pointed to a picture on the wall; "in the foreground of this beautiful picture, we have the exact spot where five minute men fell after a heroic encounter with the British, in the year—"

"Oh, Bet, do stop; it's too horrible. Can't we cut?" There was a moment's silence.

"We cut one lecture," Polly said with meaning.

"And we promised Mrs. Baird we'd never do it again," Lois finished for her.

Polly whistled softly and reached for her sweater.

"Where are you going?" Betty demanded.

"For a walk, and I don't want any company," Polly replied, going out quietly and shutting the door.

Lois and Betty were too surprised to speak. And when they had recovered sufficiently to go out and follow Polly, it was too late, for Polly had chosen the most unlikely spot for her walk.

At dinner that night, Mrs. Baird announced the lecture. It was received with respectful silence. The rest of the girls were quite as disappointed as Lois and Betty had been—Polly was the only cheerful one at the Freshman table, and Betty whispered to Lois:

"I can't make Polly out; she acts as if she were pleased."

"Poll," Lois appealed direct, "what is the matter with you, do you really think you are going to like this lecture?"

Polly smiled an inscrutable smile—"History is my favorite lesson," she said primly.

After dinner she disappeared. There would be fifteen minutes before the lecture began and she had enough to do to fill each one. She went straight to the power house. Pat was standing in the doorway, his pipe in his mouth, and an expression on his face that boded ill to all lectures.

"Beautiful evening, isn't it?" Polly greeted him.

Pat looked surprised. "Oh, you're back again. What is it you want to know now?" he asked.

"Nothing much, I just thought it would be fun to see you fix up the connection for the lantern," Polly answered idly.

"Sure, it's all fixed. I'm sorry; had I knowed you was that interested, I'd a waited."

"Oh, pshaw." Polly looked very crestfallen.

"It's an easy matter to show you how it's done, though. Come inside."

After a lengthy and voluble discourse on the one hand, and eager attention on the other, Polly asked:

"So, really, if you just pulled down that switch the lantern wouldn't work up at school?"

"Not till it was turned on again, but why—"

"Pat," Polly interrupted hastily, "don't you think it's time to go up to school? They can't begin without you."

Pat's face fell and he sighed reproachfully.

"There, I suppose you're right; I'll be getting my coat."

"Pat, do you like to work the lantern for lecture?"

"I do not; well, that's not always."

"How about tonight?"

"Tonight?" Pat hesitated, tried to keep his reserve, and then gave it up. "It's like this, Miss, tonight I made plans to go to the village, and so you can see that this lecture coming sudden like, is not, in a manner of speaking, welcome to me."

"Hard luck; I'm sorry," Polly said airily. "It can't be helped, though; I guess we'd better start." They left the power house and had gone about a hundred feet when Polly stopped.

"Gracious, Pat, I've left my Latin book in the power house. I'll have to go back for it. There goes the bell; you'd better hurry."

Professor Irvington Hale mounted the platform in Assembly room at exactly seven-fifteen. He was a young old man with a knotty forehead and very large ears. He wore horn rim glasses and he carried a black ebony pointer in one hand. Betty described him adequately when she whispered to Lois: "He's an owl."

Lois smothered a giggle and turned to Polly—They were all sitting in the front row. "Two hours of that; O dear."

Polly was occupied in watching Mr. Hale, very closely. She only said: "Oh, cheer up," and kept on watching.

"Good evening, young ladies. I—er—have the pleasure to address you this evening on New England and its historical past—" The professor was already stumbling on his way. After his opening remark he coughed, shifted his feet, and consulted a card that he held in the palm of one hand. "First picture, please," he said rather abruptly.

The lights were turned out promptly, and the girls settled down with a sigh of resignation.

They waited, no picture came; the white curtain waved ghost-like in the dark. The younger girls began to giggle nervously and then some one turned on the light. Mrs. Baird went to the back of the room.

"What's the matter, Pat, is there something wrong with the lantern?"

Pat scratched his head in solemn wonder. "Sure, there should be nothing wrong with it," he said.

"Perhaps the trouble is at the power house," Mrs. Baird suggested. "You better go as quickly as possible and find out. And in the meantime," she continued, returning to the platform, "perhaps Professor Hale will talk to us."

But Professor Hale would not, could not. He had just his lecture, all learned by heart. A picture slipped in at the wrong time would have seriously upset him. He fled from the very idea of attempting to talk against time to this room full of fluttering beribboned young ladies. He refused point-blank—

The school waited restlessly for Pat's return. It was prompt. Mrs. Baird rose as he entered, and there followed a low voiced and very lengthy explanation in which the words "wouldn't happen in a hundred years," "short circuit," and "sorry to disappoint the gentleman," entered repeatedly.

Mrs. Baird explained that it would be impossible to fix the lantern that night, and tried again to induce Professor Hale to give a short talk, but to no avail. He departed with the Spartan without another word.

"There will be no lecture tonight, girls," Mrs. Baird announced, "and you may go out as you planned to do. Don't go too far away from the house and be sure and return promptly when you hear the bell." And glancing at the clock she added, smiling: "You haven't lost much time."

It was the merriest of parties that set out a few minutes later for the old fort.

Lois and Betty tried their hardest to find out just how Polly was responsible, for responsible they knew she was, but Polly refused to say anything. Her eyes danced with fun and impishness as she insisted it was really too bad that they'd had to miss the lecture. When the others joined them Lois and Betty dropped the subject. They sang all the school songs, and did a great deal of speculating about the future. Miss Porter told story after story of college.

"It's been the jolliest and at the same time the saddest evening of the whole year," Connie declared, as they hurried home at the first sound of the bell. "Hasn't it, though; it's been so nice just being together. I don't believe we'll any of us ever forget it," Angela agreed.

Polly thought of that remark as she sat up in bed an hour later.

"I know I'll never forget it," she said to her conscience—"It really was a wonderful evening, and it couldn't have been so very wicked for me to turn off that switch. And oh dear, Pat was so funny; I know he was pleased. It was hard for him, though, having to do all the fibbing. I wonder why things you know are wrong seem right sometimes. This was the sort of thing Aunt Hannah would have said 'I'm shocked' about, but when I tell Uncle Roddy he'll only say: 'Good for you, Tiddle de Winks.' It's too much for me, I don't understand," she finished, drowsily. And in a few minutes sleep relieved her of any further need of explanation.

CHAPTER XVIII—WANTED: A MASCOT

"There will be a meeting of the big team and substitutes in classroom A at 2 o'clock this afternoon. Please be prompt," read Lois, standing in front of the bulletin board. She had finished her last exam. and was free for the rest of the week.

It was Thursday and just one week before Commencement. Mrs. Baird believed in having the examinations over before the excitement of the last days gave the girls something else to think about.

School continued, however, until three days before the close. The teachers took that time to go over the papers with the girls and have a general review.

Lois, still gazing at the notice, caught sight of her chum leaving the schoolroom and called to her:

"Hey, Polly, come here and look at this."

"Hum! Wonder what it's all about," mused Polly after she had read it. "Do you know?"

"Final preparation for Field Day, of course. Oh, Polly, if we'd only get a chance to play!" sighed Lois.

"No such good luck. You may, but I've had my chance. Why couldn't I have waited and sprained my ankle for this game, when I'm not needed!" grumbled Polly.

"What! And missed Commencement! Poll, you're crazy!"

"Well, perhaps I am. Anyhow, let's go down to Senior Alley and see if we can find Louise," suggested Polly. "I want to know what's up."

They found Louise in her room and began at once to question her.

"What are we going to have a team meeting for?" demanded Lois.

"Are any of the big team sick?" Polly added eagerly.

"I never knew such inquisitive children," answered Louise. "I knew you'd be here the minute you'd seen the notice. Can't you possess your souls in patience until 2 o'clock?"

"No, we can't possibly. Go on and tell us, *please*," begged Lois, putting both arms around Louise's neck and ruffling her hair. "We won't open our mouths," she promised.

"You know we love you an awful lot, and you might give us a tiny hint," teased Polly. "Besides, we won't go till you do."

"Imps," declared Louise, and pulling the girls down on the bed beside her and putting an arm around each, she continued: "Listen to me: to get rid of you, I'll tell you part, not all, mind, of what we are going to discuss."

"Well, go on; don't stop," prompted Polly and Lois, as Louise stopped for breath.

"Of course you know that Flora Illington's place is not filled so we have to decide definitely on another substitute to play center and—"

"You'll choose Betty," finished Polly, with a rush.

"Will you tell her today?" demanded Lois excitedly. "Oh, I am glad!"

And to show their entire approval of the idea, both girls threw their arms around their poor defenseless captain and hugged her until she called for help.

"Woh!" she exclaimed when they had finally let her go. "If I had known how you were going to treat me, I never would have told you; you've pulled my hair all down, wretches."

"Never mind that; you can put it up again. Tell us when you are going to tell Betty," urged Lois.

"We'll have to vote on it as a matter of form, but of course she'll get it. But promise me you won't breathe a word about it until I say you may."

"We promise; but won't Betty be thrilled!" laughed Polly.

The luncheon bell interrupted them and they left Louise madly fixing her hair, to join the line.

At the table Betty asked:

"What are you two so quiet about?"

Polly and Lois exchanged smiles.

"You'll see soon enough; it's about you," Polly told her, and for fear too much had been said, Lois added:

"It's something terrible!"

Betty stopped in the act of putting some tomato catsup on her croquette to demand:

"Which exam. have I flunked, or is it all of them?"

"Worse than that," answered Lois. "But you'll soon know."

At 2 o'clock the teams met in classroom A and Betty's name was put up for substitute, and as Louise had prophesied, every one voted yes. The girls all adored Betty and had been sorry to see her left out in the first election on account of the fouls she always made. But now when her name came up again and they remembered the plucky fight she had made the day of the Indoor Meet, they were only too delighted to welcome her as one of the "subs."

"Hadn't we better call her in for the rest of the meeting?" suggested Louise. "Polly, will you go and find her? Don't tell her what she's wanted for; just bring her here."

A few minutes later Betty arrived, looking very apprehensive, and Louise told her with all due form and ceremony that she had been chosen to fill Flora's place on the team.

Betty's delight knew no bounds. The girls cheered her and were very strenuous in their congratulations. It was fully fifteen minutes before the meeting came to any sort of order. When things did finally quiet down, Louise, as captain, took the chair.

"Field Day is not two weeks off," she began. "You all know that we are going to play the Fenwick School again this year and we must win."

Then looking at Polly, she added: "Please be careful and don't get any broken ankles or arms, for you may all be needed. Remember, they beat us last year."

"That was because we played on their floor and it was strange to us," spoke up Florence Guile. She had played in the game the year before and felt she must defend the team's honor. "This year we play here and we will win; you see if we don't."

At this point Nora Peters, one of the Juniors who was not on the team, knocked at the door. She had a letter in her hand and she spoke hurriedly to Louise.

"I am awfully sorry to disturb you," she said, "but I've just had a letter from one of the Fenwick girls, and I thought it might interest you. It's about the team."

"Good! Read it to us!" exclaimed half a dozen voices.

"This is the important part," began Nora as she read:

"'We have a wonderful team this year and so far we haven't had a single defeat.'"

("O Jemima!" groaned Betty.)

"'We play four other teams every year; you play only two, don't you? Our centers are great! I remember last year when your team played here how easily we beat you! I hate to say it, Nora dear, but we're going to beat you again!'"

"That's all she says about the team," Nora finished, folding up the letter. "No, wait a minute," she added. "This may interest you, too. She says:

"'We have the most adorable mascot; wait till you see him; and he's never failed us yet.'"

"Thanks, ever so much," Louise exclaimed as soon as she stopped reading. "That's valuable information. We're much obliged to your friend."

"I wouldn't have said anything about it if she hadn't bragged so," Nora answered, backing to the door. "But mind, you beat them *well*, so that I can say 'I told you so.'"

"We will, we will," cried the team with one voice.

"Now what do you think of that?" demanded Madelaine Ames, one of the guards, a tall lanky girl with straight hair.

"What did she say about a mascot?" Betty inquired eagerly.

"That they had an adorable one," replied Mary Reeves, the other guard.

88

"We ought to have one, too," chimed in Helen Reed, the jumping center. "Something original, I say; I'm tired of cats and dogs."

"Everybody think hard," suggested Louise, "and if you think of something, let me know and I'll call a meeting. We can't let them get ahead of us even in a mascot."

After a few unimportant details were discussed, the meeting broke up and the girls separated, each to think of a fitting mascot.

The next morning Lois, Betty and Polly, having finished all their exams, had the whole glorious day to themselves. Right after breakfast they disappeared into the woods and sought their favorite brook. When they reached it, they were very hot and tired, for the day was warm, and they had run all the way.

"Phew!" gasped Betty, throwing herself down beside the stream. "I'm hot."

"So am I," Polly agreed, resting her chin on her hands. "My feet, particularly. I have on these old hot gym shoes."

"Why don't we go in paddling?" suggested Lois. "It couldn't hurt us; it's so lovely and warm."

No sooner said than done. In two minutes their shoes and stockings were off and they were wading, ankle-deep, in the cool water.

"Great, isn't it?" gurgled Betty, looking down at her toes. "Ouch! Be careful of this spot; there's a sharp stone," she warned.

As Polly was about to look at the spot Betty was pointing to, a queer chattering noise up in the tree above her head caught her attention. Looking up she saw a dark brown "something" sitting on a limb of the tree.

"Look!" she whispered.

"What is it?" gasped Lois when she had seen.

"Why, don't you know?" Betty demanded. "We've simply got to get it; I'll climb up the tree."

"Be careful not to scare it," cautioned Polly.

But there was no fear of that, for as soon as Betty reached the limb occupied by "it," there was a scuffle, and she felt something land on her shoulder.

"I've got it, safe and sound," she called to the girls below.

"Look how thin it is," said Lois when Betty was again on terra firma. "Let's take it back to school and feed it, it must have run away."

"Of course we will—the darling—and—Oh, Polly, Lo, why didn't we think of it the minute we saw it? We'll have it for a mascot!"

That afternoon there was a very important team meeting in one of the classrooms. It lasted just a few minutes, but when the girls came out they were all smiling very mysteriously, and they seemed to be delighted about something.

There was a good deal of smuggling of food into the cellar, of which Mrs. Baird had given Betty the key.

For the remaining few days before Field Day, every time one of the team met Betty, Lois or Polly, they would inquire very mysteriously how "it" was, and before many days passed the word went round the school that Seddon Hall had discovered a worthy mascot.

CHAPTER XIX—FIELD DAY

Field Day arrived and with it the excitement known to any girl who has played in a big game of basket-ball.

"Oh, Polly, I'm so thrilled!" exclaimed Lois, putting her arm around her chum and dancing wildly down the corridor. "I'm glad my family isn't coming."

"So am I," Polly answered, thinking of Bob. "If we could only get a chance to play!"

"Hush! I don't even dare think of such a thing!"

"Well, I do, and I'll bet anything that the big team girls can't pass the ball as fast as you and Betty and I can."

"They can't. I watched last practice game and they made some dreadful mistakes with the signals. By the way, how is 'it' this morning?"

"Fine, Betty took some food to the cellar right after breakfast. The darling's really getting fat."

"Here comes Bet now. Oh, Betty, here we are!" Lois called as the third member of the trio appeared at the other end of the corridor.

"Thank goodness, I've found you," Betty answered. "All substitutes are wanted in the gym. Louise is waiting for you; hurry up."

The above conversation took place in Freshman Alley about ten o'clock in the morning. Throughout the entire school the game was the one subject that was being discussed. The girls had pinned the Seddon Hall colors on the fronts of their sailor suits, and the long green and white ribbons gave the required holiday effect.

In the gym the more ardent admirers of the team were busy with the decorations. The big Seddon Hall banner almost covered one end of the room and the other walls were hung with small school flags and streamers. Angela and Connie, both seated on the floor, were carefully polishing the handsome silver loving cup.

It was upon this scene of preparation that Betty, followed by Polly and Lois, entered.

"Here they are," she announced to Louise who, with the rest of the team, was waiting for them at the other end of the gym. "I've found them at last."

"That's good; I guess we are all here now," Louise replied. "I wanted to tell you that the Fenwick girls get here at 12.05. The teams and substitutes are all to have luncheon in the younger children's dining-room. We will have to entertain them and show them around, of course, but, girls, don't talk too much; remember, they may be trying to pump. I guess that's all I wanted to say," Louise finished, "except," she added miserably, "to remind you all to do your very best for the honor of dear old Seddon Hall."

"Of course we will!" shouted the team, and Madelaine Ames, jumping up from her seat, asked excitedly:

"Who's the finest captain in the world?"

"Louise Preston," came the hearty response.

Louise, to cover her confusion, called Betty to her and asked if "it" had been fed.

"Fed! It's been stuffed," Betty assured her. "But who has the bow for its neck?"

"I have it in my room," answered Helen Reed. "If you'll come with me I'll give it to you." And the two girls left the gym.

It had been decided that the big team should march into the gym first, followed by the substitutes, Betty leading the still mysterious mascot, and Polly and Lois carrying the huge Seddon Hall banner.

The girls left the gym to await the arrival of the visiting team after Louise had finished talking to them. At quarter past twelve they arrived, and at the first sound of the carry-all's approach, the Seddon Hall girls started cheering, and Louise, as captain, stepped forward to welcome them.

Lois, Betty and Polly moved a little to one side in order to get a good look at their opponents.

"That girl's a giant," whispered Lois, pointing at one of the Fenwick girls. "I'll bet she plays home."

"Seems to me they are all giants," Betty grumbled. "I suppose that's their mascot in that basket; well, it can't beat ours."

"Why, there are only nine of them," pointed out Polly excitedly. "That means only three 'subs.' What luck!"

"Come here, you three," called Louise from the driveway. "Some more of our substitutes," she explained as the trio shook hands all around.

As they all stood exchanging greetings, Mary Reeves whispered in Polly's ear, as she pretended to fix her hair ribbon:

"It's all over for us."

The girls finally sauntered off in groups to inspect the gym and locker rooms or to look around the grounds. Polly, Lois, and Betty had undertaken to entertain the three visiting subs and were taking them in the direction of the woods.

"Have you a mascot?" asked one of them, a fair-haired girl of about fifteen.

Polly told her that they had, and then abruptly changed the subject by asking:

"Have you had to substitute often this year?"

"No, I haven't, but May has," answered the Fenwick sub.

"Do tell us about it," Polly inquired.

May was only too anxious to have her turn in the conversation.

"It was just before Easter," she began, "and we were playing the Whitehead team. I came in the second half; the score was a tie and we couldn't make a point. The other team had a free throw on account of our foul and Jane—she's our forward—told me to watch, and when she threw her braid over her right shoulder, to throw high. Well, I watched and did as she told me, and we made a goal."

"How terribly exciting!" murmured Lois without changing a muscle of her face. "And you just won the game by a single point?"

"Yes, it was thrilling," May agreed. "Of course if Esther hadn't had to have gotten out of the game, we would have made more points; they know each other's signals so well."

"And signals make such a difference," Betty remarked, giving Polly's arm a surreptitious pinch.

Polly smiled in reply and in a few minutes excused herself.

"There is something rather important that I must attend to before luncheon," she explained.

Fifteen minutes later, on her way to the dining-room she slipped a note into Louise's hand.

"Read it when you are alone," she whispered, and this is what Louise read:

"The two forwards signal with their braids. Over the right shoulder, means throw high. Tell Madelaine and Mary to watch."

The game was scheduled to start at 3 o'clock sharp and by 2.30 the teams were all in their suits and the gym was filling up with the girls and the faculty. At the stroke of three the Fenwick team entered and marched to the opposite side of the gym, and came to a halt under a banner of yellow and white, their school colors. Two of their substitutes followed, carrying a white satin cushion on which sat a tortoise-shell cat with a big white bow on its neck. On close inspection it was discovered to have six toes on one paw, and was therefore very lucky.

As they entered, the Seddon Hall girls gave them a cheer and then sang the welcoming song, written by Angela for the occasion. There was just enough time for every one to quiet down before the home team appeared. Louise Preston led, carrying the ball, then came Florence Guile; they were the two forwards and were followed in turn by Mary Reeves and Madelaine Ames, the guards, and Grace Hampton and Alice Wentworth, the centers.

At sight of them the school set up a mighty cheer that stopped abruptly, however, as Betty, with a little brown monkey perched on her shoulder, entered, at the head of the substitutes.

The mysterious secret of the mascot was out. Seddon Hall had had many and varied animals for mascots in its time, but never before had a live monkey attended one of the Field Day games. It was fully ten minutes before the teams were able to take their places on the floor, so great was the school's delight. Had the organ grinder who had lost his pet witnessed this scene he might have felt recompensed for his loss.

When at last Miss Stuart could command silence, she blew the whistle, tossed up the ball, and the game was on.

From the very first it seemed to Polly, Lois and Betty, watching from the side lines, that they must face defeat. After the first toss-up, the Fenwick center caught the ball, passed it up the floor to her forward, and before the Seddon Hall girls could realize it, a goal was won.

After three unsuccessful attempts to get the ball away from her opponent, Grace Hampton lost her nerve and started to cry. She was a good player when all went well, but once unnerved she was practically useless for the rest of the game.

In the middle of a scrimmage the ball rolled out of bounds, and Miss Stuart called time for a minute.

"Get ready to get in the game, Polly," whispered Louise hurriedly. "You may be needed."

Polly tore off her sweater and waited. The game, after the minute's time was up, began again. Alice Wentworth played too hard in her attempt to support Grace and fouled for roughness. As the Fenwick forward prepared to throw for her basket, Louise asked to put in a substitute. Grace left the floor in tears and Polly took her place.

She played like a little fury for the rest of the first half, but to no purpose, for Alice Wentworth was now thoroughly wild and could give her no support.

"What is the matter with that girl?" groaned Betty, stamping with rage. "Can't she understand a straight signal! Oh, if they'd only let me in!"

"I can't do it all," Polly cried desperately as she dived for the ball near the line where Lois and Betty sat.

"You've got to," Lois answered. "How much longer will this half last?" she asked, turning to Betty.

"Long enough to leave no chance for us. Oh, Lo, they've made another basket!" And Betty wrung her hands in despair.

After a few minutes more of desperate struggling to keep the ball away from the other team, Miss Stuart blew the whistle, and the first half was over. The score was 5—0 in the Fenwick team's favor.

The school cheered half-heartedly, and under Connie's vigorous leadership, they sang to each member of the team in the vain hope of encouraging them. Polly was completely out of breath and Lois made her lie flat on her back and Betty forbid her talking.

After a doleful fifteen minutes the whistle blew again and the second half started. Up went the ball, and despite Polly's frantic efforts to stop it, it flew straight in the direction of the wrong goal. The fact that Madelaine and Mary knew the Fenwick signals helped considerably, for they managed to keep them from getting some baskets which they might otherwise have made. The ball seemed to be always at their end of the floor.

To the girls on the side lines it looked hopeless, when suddenly things began to happen. Alice fouled three times for roughness and was put out of the game.

"Thank goodness," Polly whispered as Betty took her place. "Don't forget the old signals."

Up went the ball again, but when it came down, it was in Polly's hands. A cry went up from the school. Betty raised her arm and put up two fingers, and Polly threw her the ball, low, swift, and straight as a die. Betty bounced it to the line and threw high to Florence, who, as she afterwards declared, was dreaming, for

93

the ball struck her full on the nose, and in a second her handkerchief was covered with blood.

Time was called and although Florence insisted that she would be all right in a minute, Miss King made her leave the floor. Louise called Lois to take her place.

"Now to show them some real playing," Betty exclaimed excitedly.

From the second the ball touched Polly's hands after the toss-up until, by a few swift passes, Louise had thrown it in the basket, the Fenwick team never had a chance at it. It sped like lightning from Polly to Betty, to Lois, to Louise. Seddon Hall had never seen such passing, and the girls showed their appreciation by prolonged cheers.

Time after time they repeated the same thing. Without doubt they had found themselves, and the Fenwick team seemed powerless to stop them.

"Yi! That's the way to do it!" shouted Betty as Louise made her fifth basket and the Fenwick captain asked to put in a substitute for center. But substitutes were of no avail; nothing could stop the Seddon Hall team. Once in a while the ball would trickle towards one of the Fenwick forwards, only to be batted back by Mary or Madelaine into Polly's or Betty's waiting hands. Once there, it was but a few swift passes, and Louise would throw it triumphantly into the basket.

Not one goal could the other team make after the first half, and when at last the game ended, the score was 9—5 in Seddon Hall's favor.

When the final whistle blew there was a mad rush, and the girls on the team were hoisted high on the shoulders of the delighted school. Some one threw the big green and white banner around Louise and put the rather frightened mascot into her arms, and singing and cheering wildly, they carried her to the other end of the gym before the table whereon the silver cup had been placed.

Polly, Lois and Betty escaped as soon as the excited girls would let them, and jumping out of their gym suits they met, a few minutes later, in Roman Alley.

"Oh, but that was a game!" gloated Betty. "Why did it ever end!"

"I nearly died of joy when you came in," Polly exclaimed. "And when Lo took Florence's place, well—" But Polly could find no words to express her feelings.

"I'll bet those Fenwick girls had the surprise of their lives. I heard Nora Peters rubbing it in to her friend that wrote her that letter. And as for mascots, wasn't their cat stupid when compared to our darling?" Lois demanded gleefully.

"Oh, there you are!" called Louise's voice from the top of the stairs. "Make room for us," she added as she came down, followed by Mary and Madelaine.

"We were just talking about the game, naturally," explained Lois. "You certainly can make baskets, O mighty Captain," she added, bowing low before Louise.

"I?" questioned Louise. "You know very well I had nothing to do with the game. You three saved the day; how am I going to thank you?"

"It was certainly a relief when you came in," sighed Madelaine. "Mary and I were almost all in."

"I'd given the game up for lost," Louise continued, putting her arm around Polly and Lois and smiling gratefully at Betty, "until you started those wonderful passes. You must have done an awful amount of practicing that I didn't dream of," she added.

The three girls looked at one another and grinned foolishly, and Betty said: "Certainly not!'

"Wasn't that a wonderful catch Mary made?" asked Lois.

"Yes; but did you see the high one Florence stopped?"

"Poor old Florence; how's her nose?"

"That Fenwick center almost killed me."

And a thousand other questions were asked and answered, and to the splash, splash of the water as it ran in their tubs, the victorious team played the game over again in words.

CHAPTER XX—THE MUSICAL

It was the morning of the musical and the day before Commencement. Lessons were over for the year, and all the girls were in a high state of holiday excitement.

Connie's name was on the program twice, the first time for a two piano piece with Nora Peters, and the second for a very difficult sonata by herself. The professor had promised that if she were encored, she might play one of her own compositions. So Connie, full of thrills, practiced night and day.

Angela, left to herself, joined forces with Betty and together with Polly and Lois they were always at the service of the Senior class. They were kept pretty busy, running errands and doing the dozen and one things that were to be done before the musical.

Just now they were sitting on the floor of the assembly room platform, waiting for orders. The Seniors had their hands full with the decorations and were transforming the dignified old room into a bower of greens and dogwood.

Madelaine Ames approached Louise with a very worried expression on her usually smiling face.

"We haven't half enough branches," she complained. "We need loads more dogwood. Can't Polly and Lois get some for us?"

"Hush!" cautioned Louise, for they were within ear-shot of the four girls. "Don't you realize that their hands mustn't be all scratched up? Ask Bet and Angela."

Madelaine crossed the platform to where the four sat in mystified silence, for they had overheard every word of the conversation between the two older girls.

"Betty," she called, "will you and Angela get us some more big branches of dogwood or apple blossoms? Those stupid Sofs brought in only little twigs. Take one of the stable boys with you to do the heavy work for you. You know about the size we want."

"Of course we will," answered Betty, "and we'll bring you the trees back if you want them," she called as they disappeared. On their way to the stables Angela said:

"I'd like to know what Lo and Poll are having their hands saved for."

As she said it, Polly and Lois, still on the platform, were wondering the same thing.

"Can't we do something for you?" Lois asked presently, trying to look unconscious.

"Yes, if you will," Louise answered. "I'm worried to death about my Commencement dress; it hasn't come yet. Will you go down to the express-room and see if there's a package for me?"

"If there is, hadn't we better open it and shake the wrinkles out of your dress?" suggested Polly.

"Do, please, and I'll love you even more than I do now," promised Louise.

The box had arrived, and as the two girls untied it and took out the countless wads of tissue-paper, they discussed the subject uppermost in their minds.

"What did Louise mean about our hands, Lo?" Polly demanded.

"Perhaps it's something to do with the musical," answered Lois, slowly smoothing out the creamy white sleeve.

"They'd hardly be so particular about that," mused Polly, "and yet it couldn't be anything to do with Commencement."

"N-no." Lois hesitated as she crumpled up a piece of tissue-paper into a tight ball. "Still, I can't help thinking that no one has been chosen to carry the ribbons on Commencement."

"But we couldn't do that," Polly objected. "We're Freshmen and you know you told me they always choose two girls from their sister class."

"They always have, but everything is so upside down this year that nothing would surprise me. The Sofs are cross because the Seniors didn't return their party."

"Don't let's think about it. Goodness, I feel just the way I did before the sub team was chosen."

"All right. I guess we'd better go and tell Louise that her dress is here."

"I do wish we hadn't overheard anything about our hands, though, for, try as I will, I can't get it out of my head," Polly remarked as they were on their way back to the Assembly Hall.

"Cheer up, we'll soon know," Lois reminded her. As they entered the room she called:

"It's here, Louise, and it's a perfect darling. It's all foamy lace and ribbons and looks just like soda-water."

"Thank you so much," Louise said. "I'm ever so much obliged."

"By the way, as we came over the Bridge of Sighs, we saw the florist's cart in the driveway. Don't you want us to bring up the flowers?" Polly inquired.

"Oh, please do, and fix them in these," Louise replied, pointing to three large glass vases.

The arrangement of the big American beauties which were to decorate the platform occupied the girls until luncheon time.

A few minutes before the bell rang, Angela and Betty returned, laden down with dogwood and apple blossoms. When they had deposited their burden and were standing with Polly and Lois, three of the Seniors joined them. Mary Reeves was one of them, and as she put her arm on Betty's shoulder she said:

"We certainly can't thank you girls enough for all you've done, but instead of giving you a rest, we are going to ask for more. Will you be ushers for us this afternoon and see about bringing in the flowers to the girls who are to take part in the musical? All the boxes will be put in the history-room and the cards will be on them."

"All you will have to do," continued Florence Guile, "is to bring them in and give them to the girls they're for, after they have finished their stunt. Will you do it for us?" she asked, smiling.

"Certainly we will," Betty replied.

"Don't try to pretend it's a favor to you," laughed Lois. "You know we just love to do it."

"I know you are all ducks, and I don't know what we would have done without you," Florence told them just as the luncheon bell rang.

When the girls had taken their seats at the table, Polly whispered to Lois:

"You see, it's all explained. It was for the musical."

"You are all wrong," contradicted Betty, who had overheard the whisper. "It's still a mystery; you forget Angela and I are going to help this afternoon, too, and I didn't notice anybody getting excited over *our* hands."

"I never thought of that. I guess you're right, Bet," Lois agreed, and she and Polly exchanged puzzled glances mixed with a new hope.

The next couple of hours were full to overflowing. The corridors were crowded with fluffy beribboned girls all talking at once.

"Some one button me up!"

"Who took my shoe horn?"

"Tie my hair ribbon for me, please!"

"I can't find my only pair of silk stockings!" and other such demands.

About half past three the first carriages from the station that were bringing the visitors began to arrive. Every one was doing a favor for some one else, or greeting friends and relatives. Such happy excitement prevailed everywhere that the school resembled a cage of fluttering butterflies.

At four o'clock the recital began. Seddon Hall was renowned for its music. Some of the girls played remarkably well, and there were a number of beautiful voices.

Connie had to give not only one encore, but two, and it was her own composition that called forth the heartiest applause.

Polly, Lois, Angela and Betty were kept busy bringing in big bunches of violets, roses and lilies-of-the-valley. After Edith Thornton had sung two funny little Irish songs and the audience had stopped their enthusiastic applause, Louise Preston rose to give the farewell address in the name of the Seniors.

With clear well-chosen words she told of her class's love for Seddon Hall, its influence for good on all who entered it, the ever-ready sympathy of its dearly loved superior, Mrs. Baird, and ended with the regret they all felt at leaving. It was a triumph of beautiful thoughts told in beautiful English.

After the thunders of applause there was hardly a dry eye in the room, and Polly and Lois were crying quite shamelessly, as they brought in the many bouquets to their Senior president.

Suddenly every one began to talk, praise, and congratulations were in the air. The musical was over. The visitors left for the hotel in the village, where they were to spend the night so as to be on hand for Commencement. The girls returned to their corridors to change their fluffy dresses for more comfortable ones and then to wander about the hall, discussing the recital and waiting for the bell.

After dinner they walked about the grounds in small groups, singing school songs and farewells to the Seniors. When they came in they spent the rest of the evening visiting from room to room and packing trunks.

The Seniors had built a bonfire on the side of the gym farthest away from the school. As the twilight deepened, their shadows lengthened as they sat around the blaze, and their thoughts turned back to the past. They were burning their old notebooks and papers.

"Well, it's all over," sighed Madelaine Ames, throwing her history examination into the fire. "But what a year it's been!"

"We've beaten last year's class average in marks," announced a voice from the shadow. "The Spartan told me so."

"Disagreeable, funny old Spartan! I'll even miss her," murmured some one else.

"We've been popular, too, I think," mused another voice.

"Louise's name will be on the cup twice as basket-ball captain." It was Mary Reeves speaking. "And no one will ever say Field Day wasn't the finest game in years."

There was silence for a few minutes and then Madelaine said:

"Wonder what the next class will be like?"

Florence Guile was gazing into the fire.

"Not much, I'm afraid," she drawled. "They're too studious."

"I've been here four years, and it breaks my heart to leave," Louise spoke for the first time.

"It isn't as bad for you and Florence as it is for the rest of us," some one answered. "You're both going to college next spring—lucky dogs—while we will have to go in for society—awful thought."

98

"But college won't be Seddon Hall," Louise replied. "Wonder if they'll miss us?"

"The Freshmen will. Oh, what a class they're going to make when they are Seniors! I hope they all come back," Mary Reeves exclaimed.

"That reminds me—What about telling Polly and Lois about tomorrow?" demanded Louise. "Mrs. Baird said to wait until after the musical. She agrees with us that none of the 'Sofs' will do, but she doesn't want them to have time to grumble."

"We forgot all about it," Madelaine gasped. "You and Florence go and ask them now, they adore you. But hurry back," she called as the two girls started for the school.

Polly and Lois were in the latter's room amid confusion, heaps of clothes, shoes, and books. Polly was curled up on the bed brushing her hair, and Lois was sitting on the window seat, her elbow on her knee and her chin cradled in her hand. They were discussing the prospects of the next winter without the Seniors.

Polly had just given vent to a deep sigh and the words:

"It will never be quite the same without them."

And Lois was saying:

"Fancy the Senior table without Louise," when they were interrupted by a knock on the door.

"Come in," called Polly, and Florence and Louise entered the room.

"I've come to thank you two precious infants for that beautiful basket of flowers," Louise began. "It was mighty thoughtful of you, and I do appreciate it so much."

Lois and Polly were so confused by the sudden entrance of the very persons they had been talking about that they could only stammer:

"Oh, it wasn't anything, really!"

"But we've something more important than that to say," Florence announced, and then waited for Louise to break the news.

Polly and Lois exchanged glances.

"It's another favor," laughed Louise. "Do you think you could act as ribbon girls for us tomorrow?" Then pretending not to hear the joyful gasps of surprise, she continued: "You'll have to come down to church tomorrow morning when we rehearse the procession and we'll show you what to do. Will you do that for us?"

It had come, and though both girls had half expected it, it was a tremendous surprise.

"Oh, Louise, you know we'd love to do it!" cried Lois.

"It's most too good to be true," Polly exclaimed excitedly, then very solemnly she added to Florence: "To think we will really help you graduate! It's the most thrilling thing that ever happened to me in my whole life!"

99

"I'm so glad you will do it for us," smiled Florence, and turning to Louise she added: "We'd better go back to the girls. I think they'll be waiting for us. It's almost time to serenade Mrs. Baird."

Polly and Lois, left alone, could do nothing but look at each other. At last Lois gave a thoroughly contented sigh.

"Who says we're not in luck?" she asked.

"It's a perfect ending to a perfect year," replied Polly, putting her arm around her friend. "You know—"

"Hush!" whispered Lois. "They're singing!"

They opened the window and leaned far out upon the ledge. Through the warm night air came the sound of the Seniors' voices singing their last farewell, beneath Mrs. Baird's window, in accordance with the old Seddon Hall custom.

CHAPTER XXI—COMMENCEMENT DAY

The sun was just peeping over the red-tiled roof of the gym, as Polly and Lois stole softly out of the house and walked slowly in the direction of the woods. The day was warm and clear with the wonderful freshness of early morning. The ground was covered with millions of cobwebs and sparkling dewdrops that danced in the sunshine.

"Commencement Day at last," Polly began, speaking in a subdued whisper, for they were still near the school windows.

"It couldn't have been more glorious," replied Lois. "I think I would have died if it had dared to rain."

They walked on a little way in silence, and then Polly said very seriously:

"It's our last day together. I'm glad you thought of this walk. We probably won't have another chance to be alone."

"I know," returned Lois. "Polly, I can't bear to think of this summer without you."

"Oh, don't remind me of it!" Polly pleaded. "Think how I'll miss you. We can write, of course, but let's cheer up. We mustn't spoil this beautiful morning by getting the blues."

They linked arms and continued their walk. The seriousness of their talk had caused them to halt in the middle of the path.

"Where will we go?" questioned Lois.

"We've time to walk as far as the brook before breakfast," Polly suggested, "and we can say good-by to all the dear old spots on the way."

The brook was visited, as were all the other places, the crow's-nest, the old wall, the ruin, and the rest of the landmarks that were dear to the heart of every Seddon Hall girl.

On the whole it was not a very cheerful walk, and when the girls returned to school in time to join the line for breakfast, they were rather sad and quiet. It was not long, however, before they caught the general spirit of excitement that prevailed and were as jolly as the rest.

"What time do you want us to practice, Louise?" Polly called as she caught sight of the busy Senior president in the corridor after breakfast.

"We are going to leave here for church at ten o'clock sharp. Be ready and wait outside Mrs. Baird's office for us," Louise answered as she hurried past.

Polly and Lois were ready and waiting many minutes before it was time to go, and it seemed hours to them before the Seniors assembled and Mrs. Baird gave the word to start. They walked hurriedly down the steep hill which leads to the village and then on to the little old church covered with ivy, located at the farthest end of the main street.

"Do let's sit down and rest a minute," said Mrs. Baird, dropping into one of the last pews and fanning herself with her handkerchief. "It's certainly a glorious day, but it's a very warm one, too."

Louise insisted that she could direct them sitting down as well as standing, so the rehearsal began. Polly and Lois were told how to manage the white satin ribbons, and the Seniors practiced the Commencement hymn.

"You see, my dears," Mrs. Baird explained to Polly, "the whole school marches in first, every one taking their place; they are followed by the faculty and visitors. When they are all seated you and Lois take the ribbons, which will be fastened to the last pews, and walk slowly up the aisle. You are followed by the Seniors, and you wait until they have received their diplomas and the service is over, then you follow them out, and the rest of the school follows you."

"It's just like a wedding, isn't it?" Lois questioned. "I think I understand."

Mrs. Baird smilingly agreed that it was, and they went through it once more to be sure.

"Isn't it solemn?" whispered Polly. "Look out, your ribbon's twisted."

"Thanks; now it's all right," Lois replied. "Doesn't Louise look sweet this morning?" she inquired as they separated to stand on either side of the aisle.

Polly could only nod in reply, which she did vigorously.

The Seniors walked up slowly and took their places, and after a few last words from Mrs. Baird, the rehearsal was over.

Louise walked back to school between Polly and Lois.

"I've been wondering," she began as they sauntered along the lazy village street, "whether you two would like to come and visit me for a while this summer. We have a big camp up in the Adirondacks, and I think you would have a good time. How about it?"

"Louise, you duck!" cried Polly and Lois in one breath. "We'd adore it. Oh, what a lark!"

"My small cousin Frances is always with us in the summer, and I'm sure you'll get along famously together," Louise told them, smiling rather mysteriously, and she added emphatically: "Yes, I'm *sure* you'll get along famously."

For the rest of the walk up the dusty hill she described the cabin in the heart of the woods, the funny guides, and spoke vaguely but frequently of Frances.

On discussing the invitation a little later after Louise had left them, Polly exclaimed:

"Won't it be a lark? I do hope we can go. Don't you love the idea?"

And Lois answered slowly:

"Yes, all except Frances. I suppose she's a nice enough girl, but I wish she wasn't going to be there."

"Why, we needn't pay any attention to her," Polly replied. "But let's find Bet. We haven't seen her all day."

They started off in search and presently found her playing with Vic (the team's mascot had been named Victor after the Field Day game, and called Vic for short), on the steps of the gym.

"Hello!" she called, as she caught sight of them. "I've been wondering where you were."

"Why, we've been practicing with the ribbons in church," replied Polly, forgetting that Betty had not heard of them being chosen by the Seniors.

"You! Ribbons!" Betty was overcome with surprise. "Well, you might have told a fellow. Jove, you are in luck!"

"I entirely forgot you didn't know. Florence and Louise asked us last night. Isn't it wonderful? I know I'll laugh, though," confided Lois, "or cry."

"Do both," advised Betty. "I'm going to make a face at you as you go down the aisle. Stop that, Vic, you wicked monkey!" she commanded, as the mascot made a playful dab at her hair ribbon.

"What's to become of Vic this summer?" demanded Polly. "Somebody has to take care of him."

"He's ours; we found him," Betty declared. "Poor old Vic. What do you say about it?" she added, scratching the monkey's ear.

As they stood discussing his future, Vic noticed a familiar figure coming down the stable road. It was Tony, one of the Seddon Hall gardeners, and a special friend of his. He had taken care of him ever since Field Day.

As if to answer their question for them, the little monkey jumped from Betty's lap, ran swiftly along the ground, and bounded to Tony's shoulder.

"The problem is solved," laughed Betty. "Tony will take care of him. Tony," she called, and the Italian came up to the steps, smiling sheepishly.

Of course he was delighted at the idea of having Vic to himself all summer, and promised to take the very best of care of him.

"You leave me your address," he said, "and I write sometime how he is."

So it was arranged. The three girls said good-by to their mascot, who was borne away on Tony's shoulder.

The rest of the day whizzed by on wings of excitement. Every one was everywhere at once. Visitors arrived in carriage loads. Those who were already there wandered through the halls trying to find the particular girl they wanted, and time was flying.

Uncle Roddy met Dr. and Mrs. Farwell in New York and brought them up in his car. They were all standing in the reception-room talking to Mrs. Baird, as Polly and Lois came down the stairs.

"Why, there's your uncle, Polly, and he's with mother and dad," exclaimed Lois, catching sight of the three in the doorway.

They were soon exchanging greetings, and Polly had time to wonder why Bob hadn't come.

"We simply must leave you," Lois said, after they had talked for a few minutes. "We are awfully busy. You know, we are to carry the ribbons for the Seniors, and we have to be in church ahead of the rest."

"We'll meet you right after the service," called Polly, as they both disappeared down the corridor.

"Well, that was short and sweet," laughed Uncle Roddy, looking after them. "They're not overgenerous with their society, are they?"

"What a darling Polly is!" Mrs. Farwell returned. "And you say she has no other relatives besides you."

"Not one. Isn't that a dreadful responsibility for a bachelor?" Uncle Roddy replied.

"Perhaps I can help you," Mrs. Farwell said. "I would love to have her with Lois as much as possible."

The bell for the guests to go to church interrupted their conversation, and they went outside to find the motor.

The Commencement exercises were a great success. The Seniors all looked beautiful and made their relatives and friends very proud of them. Polly and Lois managed the Ribbons without any trouble and added greatly to the dignity of the scene.

Once during the chaplain's short address they caught Betty's eye just as he said "certainly not," and they almost laughed. It was a terrible moment, but the loud "amen" that soon followed saved the day and gave them a chance to snicker without being noticed.

"I'll kill Bet for that," whispered Polly, as they walked sedately down the aisle after the Seniors at the close of the service.

But the excitement of leaving made her forget her threat, when fifteen minutes later she and Lois and Betty met in the latter's room.

"There, I think I've packed everything," sighed Betty. "Jemima, how I hate to leave!"

"'When shall we three meet again?'" quoted Lois. "Sometime this summer, I hope."

"It would be a lark if we could be together some of the time, wouldn't it?" mused Polly. "Perhaps we can. Who knows?"

"I am going down, now," announced Betty. "I want to say hello to Mr. Pendleton. If I don't see you two again, why good-by and don't forget to write." And she was gone. Not for worlds would she have displayed the emotion she felt.

103

Polly and Lois stole down to Senior Alley for a last good-by to Louise and dragged her down to meet their families. Then after much kissing, giving of addresses, shouted last messages and promises to come back, they finally found themselves in Uncle Roddy's motor.

They were both silent for a few minutes and their eyes were misty as they watched the towers of Seddon Hall grow fainter and fainter, until they entirely disappeared.

"We'll have to say good-by to each other next," whispered Lois.

"Don't!" answered Polly, with just a little catch in her voice. "I can't bear to think of it, Lo."

Then it was that they realized that Uncle Roddy was talking.

"So," he was saying, "if Mrs. Farwell will be contented in that sleepy old town, there's the big house at her service and the children will be together."

"Of course I'll be contented. It will be a wonderful summer," answered Mrs. Farwell.

"Capital!" spoke up the Doctor. "Roddy and I can come up for the week ends and have some fishing."

The two girls looked at each other in astonishment.

"We will be together after all," exclaimed Polly excitedly.

"But where?" Lois demanded.

"At my old home," Polly explained. "Just to think I'll see my precious dogs again!"

They parted hours later, after a very happy drive spent in discussing plans for the summer. It was parting, of course, but as Lois reminded every one delightedly: "It was only until next week."

That night Uncle Roddy noticed that Polly was looking very thoughtful as she sat on the arm of his chair.

"What's the matter, Tiddle-dy-winks?" he inquired, pulling her down on his knee and patting her shoulder. "What are you thinking about?"

"I'm thinking," replied Polly slowly, "how sorry I am it's all over. It's been the happiest year of my life."

"But that's only so far," laughed Uncle Roddy. "You've still a number of years to come, I hope."

"But can they ever be as happy as this one?" Polly asked.

"If I have anything to say about it, each year will be happier than the last, dear child, and now, good night." And Uncle Roddy gave her a hearty kiss.

So Polly, with Uncle Roddy's promise still ringing in her ears, fell asleep at the close of that eventful year, not thinking regretfully of the past, but dreaming happily of the joys to come.

THE END

CPSIA information can be obtained at www.ICGtesting.com
Printed in the USA
BVOW04s2228131114

375100BV00022B/217/P